TOPZ SECRET STORIES

ONE TOO
MANY FOR
Benny

Alexa Tewkesbury

CWR

Published 2012 by CWR, Waverley Abbey House, Waverley Lane, Farnham, Surrey GU9 8EP, UK. Registered Charity No. 294387. Registered Limited Company No. 1990308.

See back of book for list of National Distributors.

All Scripture references are from the Good News Bible, copyright © American Bible Society 1966, 1971, 1976, 1992, 1994.

Concept development, editing, design and production by CWR

Illustrations: Mike Henson at CWR

Printed in Croatia by Zrinski

ISBN: 978-1-85345-915-3

Hi there!
I'm Clyde - I'm in the Dixons Gang.

You might have heard of us. There's me and my mates, Rick and Kevin, and we all live on the Dixons Estate, in Holly Hill.

There's not that much to do in Holly Hill so we like to hang out together. The best places are the shopping centre and the park – there's lots of room there to play football or ride a bike.

Sometimes we run into the Topz Gang. 'Topzies' we call them just cos it bugs them. They're really annoying – they always seem to be talking about God and I don't get it. Us Dixons, we're cool. But Topz, they're just a waste of space.

And as if it's not bad enough that those Topzies are forever hanging around, now Ashley's moving in, too.

That's what this story is all about ...

3

Hi! We're the Topz Gang –

Topz because we all live at the 'top' of something …
either in houses at the top of the hill, at the top of the
flats by the park, even sleeping in a top bunk counts!

We are all Christians, and we go to Holly Hill School.

We love Jesus, and try to work out our faith in God
in everything we do – at home, at school and with our
friends. That even means trying to show God's love to
the Dixons Gang who tend to be bullies, and can be a
real pain!

If you'd like to know more about us, visit our website
at www.cwr.org.uk/topz You can read all about us,
and how you can get to know and understand the Bible
more by reading our *Topz* notes, which are great fun,
and written every two months just for you!

One

From the moment Ashley Bicton could hold a crayon, she was a scribbler.

She scribbled on everything. Not the things she wasn't meant to scribble on, like walls and library books and the wooden headboard on her bed. But on used envelopes. On scraps of paper. On old magazines put out for recycling.

Ashley got through countless colouring books, too. She didn't fill in the pictures beautifully with her crayons. She was still trying to learn not to go over the drawing outlines. And sometimes her trees were orange and her skies were green with purple clouds. But what did it matter? Her mother would still smile proudly as she flicked through the finished pages.

'Would you believe it?' she'd say. 'Proper little artist you are, aren't you, Ashley? Isn't she, Rob?' she'd add to Ashley's dad. 'She's a proper little artist is our daughter.'

Ashley loved storybooks, too. Her mum and dad both sat down and read to her every day. Her favourite story was *The Three Little Pigs* read to her by her dad, Rob. Ashley would growl like the wolf. She'd huff and she'd puff as she blew down the little pigs' houses made of straw and sticks. Then she'd start giggling and chuckling as she watched her dad being the wolf trying to blow down the house of bricks. Rob's cheeks would grow redder and redder, and he'd get more and more breathless.

Finally he'd say, 'Go on, Ashley, you have a go.'

Then Ashley would be the wolf again, puffing and blowing and grunting. But nothing could shift that sturdy old house of bricks.

Ashley quickly knew the words to the story so well that she didn't need it to be read to her. She could easily tell it to herself, following the pictures in the book. But she didn't want to. The fun of the tale was hearing her dad wheezing like the wolf and squealing like the scared little piggies. For Ashley, that was the best part.

Until one particular evening when everything changed.

Ashley bounced into her bed the way she usually did. Her skin felt fresh and clean from her bath. Her mouth was all minty with toothpaste.

Rob perched down next to her and asked quietly, 'What's it to be, then?'

'*Three Little Pigs*, Daddy!' Ashley squealed, sounding a bit like a little pig herself.

But as Rob started reading, Ashley thought her dad's voice sounded different from normal. He kept pausing and swallowing. He didn't seem to be enjoying the story as much as usual. Ashley fidgeted and giggled and peered into her dad's face. But before the wolf had even begun to blow down that first house, the one made of straw, her dad just stopped.

'Come on, Daddy,' Ashley said, giving Rob's sleeve a little tug.

Finally, Rob sniffed and murmured, 'Actually, Ashley, erm … I've got a bit of a headache. I'm not sure I can carry on with this right now.'

That's when Ashley noticed that Rob's eyes were glistening. The little girl frowned.

'Are you crying, Daddy?' she asked.

Rob didn't answer.

'Have you hurt yourself?' Ashley went on. 'I cry when I hurt myself, don't I? Have you hurt yourself, Daddy?'

Rob shook his head. 'No, darling, I'm fine. Just a bit sleepy, that's all. Do you mind if we finish now?' he smiled, reaching out and tickling Ashley's tummy so that she chuckled. 'Look at you. All tucked up and ready for a good night's sleep. We'll do the story tomorrow instead.'

But they didn't.

They never read that particular story together ever again, because the very next day, Ashley's dad moved out of their house. Ashley had to say goodbye to him.

Not forever. Not for more than a few days the first time, because Rob called in again at the weekend to take his daughter out. He called for Ashley every weekend for a long while afterwards, too.

What Ashley had to say goodbye to forever was their old way of life.

'Your mum thinks it's better this way,' Rob tried to explain. 'Better if you and she have your house together and I have my own place. And as soon as I'm sorted out, you can come and stay. Every weekend if you want. You're my little girl. My special little girl and I love you and I'm so proud of you. When it comes to blowing down houses, you could certainly give that old wolf a run for his money!'

Ashley couldn't understand why everything had to change. She was too small, not even four years old. But she enjoyed her days out with her dad.

Before Rob moved into a flat of his own, they mostly did things together in town. On dry days, they went for walks in the park. Ashley's dad pushed her on the swings and clambered up to the top of the slide steps behind her so that she couldn't fall. Then Ashley would zoom down the slide, squealing. When her dad followed after her, making faces and waving his hands, she giggled delightedly.

Sometimes they went on bus rides or to the library or the toyshop. And Ashley had a favourite place – The Fat Cat Café. There, her dad treated her to milkshakes and ice cream until she felt as full as a fat cat herself. One of the ladies who worked behind the counter usually popped over to their table for a chat. Her face was round and red, and always smiley.

'You're a lucky girl going out with your dad, aren't you, Ashley?' she'd beam. 'I remember going to a café sometimes with my dad when I wasn't much older than you are now. He'd get me a glass of orange juice and a chocolate éclair. Stuffed with cream those éclairs were, let me tell you! They were my downfall, too. Look at the size of me now!' And she'd laugh loudly and ruffle Ashley's long, curly, blond hair.

There was another lady who used to talk to them in the café. Sometimes, if Rob and Ashley were in there first, she'd bustle in from the street, come over and seat herself at their table. Sometimes they'd walk in and she'd already be sitting there with a mug of coffee in front of her.

Then, 'There's Cathy,' Ashley's dad would say. 'Let's go and join her, eh?'

Ashley didn't mind sitting with Cathy. Cathy always talked to her. She was always kind. Often, she'd have a book in her bag for Ashley to look at. Other times, the three of them might play 'I Spy'. Cathy always helped Ashley out by giving her big clues. When Cathy was in the café, Rob seemed happier, too. He laughed a lot. He told jokes. He looked more the way he used to when he read Ashley bedtime stories.

All the same, the special times for Ashley – the *really* special times – were when she and her dad shared a table at The Fat Cat Café on their own.

Of course, it was a bit different on rainy 'Daddy days', as Ashley called them. Rob didn't want his little girl to get soaked. That's when they'd go back to the flat where her dad was staying with a friend from work. He tried not to take Ashley there much as it wasn't his own place. It was too small and there wasn't anywhere for them to go where they could be out of the way. Rob didn't even have his own bedroom. He just slept on the sofa.

When at last Rob did manage to get a flat of his own, it was different. It could rain as much as it liked. He and Ashley had their own space. But they still made regular visits to The Fat Cat Café, and more often than not Cathy would meet them there.

Then, one Saturday, when Ashley's dad unlocked the door to his flat, Cathy was waiting for them inside. How had she got in when Rob had the key? She didn't look like a visitor, Ashley thought. She'd taken her shoes off.

'Shall I put the kettle on?' Cathy said cheerfully. 'And I think, young lady,' she added to Ashley as she disappeared into the kitchen, 'that there might be some blackcurrant in one of these cupboards for you.'

Ashley had once thought she would always be with her mum and her dad, all living together in one house. Now she imagined it was this *new* life that was here to stay.

But it seemed to her that hardly had her dad got settled into his own flat than he was moving on again. And this time, he wasn't moving on his own.

'Do you want any more chocolate sauce?' Rob said to Ashley one day as they sat in the window of The Fat Cat Café.

Ashley shook her head. She couldn't speak. Her mouth was too full of ice cream. It oozed out at the corners and dribbled down her chin.

'You mucky pup!' Rob grinned, dabbing at her face with a paper napkin. Then, 'You do like Cathy, don't you, Ashley?' he asked.

Just before she crammed another spoonful of ice cream into her mouth, Ashley mumbled, 'Yes.' Then she concentrated on the bowl in front of her.

'That's good,' her dad said. 'That's very good. She's been a good friend to me. And to you; she thinks you're fantastic. It's not been easy these last few months, has it, and … well, she's been great.'

As far as grabbing Ashley's attention was concerned, the ice cream was still winning.

'Anyway, Ashley,' her dad stumbled on, 'the thing is I'm really glad that you like Cathy. *Really* glad. Because actually … I love her. I do, I love her. And, in a while, when things are all sorted out with your mum, Cathy and I … well, Cathy and I are going to get married.'

Ashley stopped eating. Not because of what her dad had just told her, but because by now she'd emptied her bowl. Something like a scowl crept across her face.

'Does that mean we won't be coming to The Fat Cat on our own ever again?' she muttered.

'Of course not!' her dad laughed. Rob had been so anxious about breaking this news to his daughter. How would she take it? What would she say? But was that really all Ashley was bothered about? Still being able to have special time alone together? 'We're going to have lots of special time together!' Rob went on. 'Just you and me, I promise. But …'

He hesitated. The girl in front of him was so small. Her fourth birthday was getting close but it was still several weeks away. Rob couldn't really expect her to understand what he was about to say, but he knew he had to tell her anyway.

'When we have our special times, Ashley,' he began, 'it probably isn't going to be at The Fat Cat for much longer. Or at the flat. Or anywhere here. You see, Cathy's been wanting to move back to be near her parents again. They live in a place called Holly Hill. It's a bit of a journey from here but it's lovely. Beautiful park. Lots of children around, just like you. So, I've managed to get a new job there and in a little while, we're going to be moving.'

'What, me too?' Ashley asked. 'And Mummy?'

'Actually, Ashley,' Rob replied as gently as he could, 'it's just going to be Cathy and me. You'll still be living here with your mum. But you're going to come and stay with us,' he went on quickly. 'I've talked it all through with Mummy. It'll be much better than staying in the flat. I'm going to try to find a place where you can have your own bedroom.'

He watched his daughter's frowning face. Ashley didn't speak. She wasn't even looking at her dad any more. Her eyes were fixed on the empty ice cream bowl on the table in front of her.

No, thought Ashley's dad, this was never going to be easy.

Two

'Are we going to your house now, Daddy?' Ashley asked one Saturday. It was the first time she'd seen her dad since he'd moved away to Holly Hill.

'Not today, Ashley,' her dad answered. 'It's all still a bit of a muddle. Cathy and I can barely find each other for boxes! And your room's the worst of the lot! But as soon as we're straightened out, you'll be our first visitor, I promise. I'll get it all arranged with Mummy. Now,' he said, his eyes twinkling, 'I think it's time for ice cream at The Fat Cat, don't you?'

Ashley wasn't very chatty, so Rob talked on. 'Do you know, it only took me two hours in the car to get here from Holly Hill. That's nothing, is it? It's not even one whole morning. We're practically living next door to you!'

He gave Ashley's hand a little squeeze. Ashley still said nothing, so Rob switched to something he was sure his daughter would want to talk about. 'How's all your drawing and colouring coming on? I haven't seen anything for a while. Have you got a new book to show me?'

This time, Ashley shook her head. 'Don't do colouring now.'

Rob raised his eyebrows. 'No colouring?' he said. 'But you love your colouring.'

For some reason she didn't understand, Ashley hadn't done much colouring for weeks. Months even. Not since her dad had moved out of their house. She just hadn't felt like it. Her scribbles had got fewer and fewer until one day, they'd stopped altogether.

When her mum first noticed, she didn't think much of it. In some ways it was a relief not having to keep buying new colouring books. It saved her some money. But after a while, it seemed odd. Not very Ashley-like. Ashley's mum knew she must be upset about her dad not living with them any more. She just hoped that, because she was so little, she'd get used to it quite quickly. As long as she still saw her dad, the new arrangement should fast become a way of life, shouldn't it? She missed her scribbler, though. Her little artist.

But Ashley hadn't given up on pencils and crayons altogether. She'd been learning to write letters and numbers at her pre-school. Soon, she could write her name. She *loved* writing her name. She'd sit at one of the tables in the large church hall next to a box of crayons, carefully forming the letters. While the other children were doing jigsaws or building plastic brick towers or playing with play dough, Ashley would be practising her name. She'd write it over and over and over again in different coloured crayon. She liked the way the letters made patterns on the page.

And the more times she wrote them on the same sheet, the less they looked like letters. They were just shapes; strange and pointy, or curved and flowing.

Ashley grew to like writing much more than colouring in pictures.

Before long, she could write other words, too, not just her name. She could even write in short sentences. They weren't always spelt properly, but when she started at primary school, her teacher was still very impressed.

'You must have worked so hard with her,'

Miss Coulson said to her mum.

'No!' Ashley's mum laughed. 'It's nothing to do with me. Or her dad. She's just always got a pencil or a crayon in her hand.'

Ashley found that writing words down helped her when she felt sad. They didn't have to make sense. It was just putting them onto paper that made her feel better. She couldn't explain why.

And there was something else Ashley couldn't explain.

Her dad and Cathy had been living in Holly Hill for almost a year. Rob would drive up on a Saturday morning and collect her. Then he'd drive back to Holly Hill where Ashley would spend the rest of Saturday and most of Sunday. Not every weekend, but as many as Rob could manage. In the school holidays, sometimes Ashley was able to stay a little longer. She had a bedroom of her own, just as her dad had said she would. They were happy times. Fun times. The three of them all enjoyed being with each other. There didn't seem to be anything missing.

So why was it, Ashley wondered, that on this particular Saturday, her dad told her that he and Cathy were having a baby?

A little boy apparently.

Why did they want a little boy when they'd got her?

'How about that, Ashley?' beamed her dad. 'A brand-new little brother for you. Very soon, too. Brilliant news, eh?'

The next evening, when Ashley was home again and her dad was driving back to Holly Hill, she pulled some paper and a pencil out of her chest of drawers. She put the paper on the chest top and wrote:

Daddy giving me a **brother.** Dont want him.

Ashley had no idea what 'very soon' meant. For a long while after Rob had told her the news, there seemed to be no sign of a baby. Ashley knew it was growing in Cathy's tummy. She knew that sometimes Cathy was resting in bed when she arrived for her weekend visits.

'It's hard work growing a baby inside you,' her dad would say.

But otherwise, nothing seemed to change.

Then one Saturday, Ashley followed Rob in through the front door and almost walked straight into a large, flat, rectangular cardboard box. It was leaning against the hall wall.

'Oops!' Rob laughed. 'Sorry, Ashley! I should have said, "Mind the cot!"'

'What cot?' Ashley asked.

'The cot for your little brother,' smiled Rob. 'Cathy and I went and bought it this week. It's in there,' and he tapped the cardboard box. 'That's my next job. Putting it together. Little chap'll be here soon.'

There was that word again, Ashley thought. 'Soon'. What did it mean? How long was 'soon'? Today? Tomorrow? When exactly was this baby arriving? One question led to another.

And then the biggest one of all crashed through Ashley's head: *which room was the baby going to sleep in?*

Her dad's house only had two bedrooms. Rob and Cathy slept in one, and Ashley slept in the other when she came to stay. Ashley liked her room here. The walls and ceiling were painted a soft, pinky-lilac. The curtains were lilac, too, with funny blue blobs, and the carpet was beige. Beside her bed was a little, round, blue rug and her duvet was tucked inside a white cover with a pattern of brightly coloured flowers. She'd chosen it herself. There was a shelf on one wall holding a few picture books. Some were Ashley's own from home, and her dad had bought her a few from charity shops to keep in Holly Hill. A small, white-painted wardrobe stood against one wall. In here her dad would hang the clothes Ashley's mum had packed for him to bring. There were several cuddly toys, too, arranged along the bed.

The room was just right. Just right for *her*, Ashley thought. So, where was the bedroom for the baby? When Rob had stayed in his friend's flat, he didn't have a room of his own. He'd slept on the sofa. But Rob and Cathy had bought a cot, so they obviously didn't mean for the *baby* to sleep on the sofa.

Ashley didn't ask her dad straightaway. She kept turning the question over and over in her mind. Perhaps there was another room in the house she knew nothing about. Somewhere tucked away behind a door she hadn't found yet. Or perhaps the baby would sleep in someone else's house. After all, Ashley slept in a different house at the weekends, didn't she? It might be her dad's house, but it was still different to her usual home.

Once she'd decided that this was the most likely answer, Ashley asked, 'Where's the baby's house, Daddy?'

Rob looked at her in surprise. 'What do you mean?'

'The baby needs a bedroom and there isn't one. Where's the house with his bedroom in?'

Rob gave a short laugh that ended abruptly as he looked into his daughter's eyes. He could see that his little girl was deadly serious.

'The baby's not going to sleep in another house, Ashley,' he explained. 'He's going to sleep here with us. This will be his home. When he first comes out of hospital – while he's still really new and tiny – he's going to be in our bedroom. Mine and Cathy's. Then, when he gets a little bit bigger, well ...'

Rob hesitated.

Ashley hadn't taken her eyes from her dad's face. Suddenly he looked awkward, Ashley thought. The skin on Rob's cheeks had a pink tinge as if they were getting hot. Ashley's face went pink like that when she'd been running about outside.

'Are you hot, Daddy?' Ashley asked. 'Why are you hot?'

'I'm not hot.' Rob shook his head. 'I'm trying to explain that when your little brother's bigger, you're right, he will need a bedroom. This is only a small house so what's going to happen is that … he's going to need to share *your* room for a while. You'll hardly notice it, Ashley. You only sleep there one night a week in any case. The rest of the time, you've got your own room at home. All the space you like.'

Ashley said nothing in reply. She didn't nod. She didn't even blink.

'You do understand, don't you?' her dad went on. 'I'm really sorry we haven't got more space. I never meant for you to have to share your room. But it won't be for long, you'll see. As soon as I can, I'm going to get us all a bigger place. As *soon* as I can, really.'

There was that word again. 'Soon'. Ashley didn't like it. She didn't understand 'soon'. She couldn't trust it. It meant a baby was arriving some time, but when? It meant she wouldn't have her own bedroom in her dad's house any more, but when? It meant everything was changing, yet again … **but when?**

Back at home in her other bedroom, Ashley went to her chest of drawers. She grabbed her box of crayons and a small, green exercise book. Her mum had given it to her. If she wasn't buying colouring books any more, she felt she could afford the odd exercise pad. She wanted to encourage Ashley's writing. Miss Coulson at school had said she was very advanced for her age.

Ashley flicked the book open. Each white page had

pale blue lines running across it for her to write her letters on. The lines were quite widely spaced, but even so, Ashley couldn't always fit her words on them neatly yet. She didn't mind. All that mattered was the letters and the words themselves, and the patterns they made. Keeping to the lines wasn't important.

Kneeling down on her bed, Ashley pulled the lid off the box of crayons and fished inside. She picked out two colours: black and purple. Starting with the black, she wrote the word 'soon' on the blank page resting open in front of her. Next to it on the top line, there was just room for her to write it again. So she did, this time in purple.

Ashley did the same thing all the way down the page. When she'd finished, she gazed at the two different coloured columns of 'soons'. She liked how they looked. She liked the way there were no sharp letters, only curvy ones.

But as for the word itself – 'soon' – no matter how long she stared at it, she still had no idea what it actually meant.

19

Three

When 'soon' finally arrived, Ashley and her mum found out through a phone call. It was a Friday evening.

The telephone rang as Ashley's mum was packing her bag for the trip to her dad's the next day. Ashley heard her mum run downstairs to answer it while she was brushing her teeth. She put her toothbrush back in the glass on the windowsill. Then she rinsed and dried her hands before trotting across the landing to her bedroom.

The bag with her spare clothes inside was still open on her bed. Ashley could hear her mum's voice as she spoke on the phone, but she wasn't listening to what she said. Instead, she looked at the books stacked side by side in her bookcase. After a moment, she pulled one of them out. Then she shoved the bag a little further along the bed to make more room, and perched down next to it.

But she didn't get further than the first page. She heard footsteps on the stairs and in a moment her mum was standing in the doorway.

'That was Daddy,' her mum said.

Ashley didn't answer. She just waited for her mum to tell her why her dad had rung. Stepping over towards the bed, her mum lifted the bag onto the floor and sat down beside her.

'Ashley,' she continued softly, 'Daddy's not going to be able to come this weekend after all.'

Again Ashley said nothing.

'The baby's come, Ashley,' she went on. 'Daddy and Cathy's baby boy. But, the trouble is, he's come too soon.'

Too soon? Ashley frowned instantly. What did that mean? She knew the baby was supposed to be coming 'soon'. So what was 'too soon'? How could that happen? How could a baby arrive 'too soon'?

Ashley's mum saw her face change and immediately took hold of her small hands and held them in her own.

'It's all right, sweetheart,' she said, trying to give her daughter a reassuring smile. 'It happens sometimes. Some babies are in such a hurry to be born that they arrive early. Sounds like this little one couldn't wait. Six weeks early he is. He's fine, though. He's in hospital being looked after, so there's no need for you to worry.'

'I'm not worrying,' Ashley answered. 'When's Daddy coming?'

'Well, that's the thing, Ashley,' her mum explained. 'Daddy's not going to be able to come for you tomorrow now. He needs to be at the hospital.'

'Why? You said the baby's being looked after.'

'He is. But … well, Daddy wants to be there, too. In case the baby or Cathy need him. He says he'll come as soon as he can. Maybe even next weekend. Let's wait and see, shall we?'

But the next weekend came and went and Rob didn't arrive.

'The baby's having a few problems,' Ashley's mum said. 'Because he arrived early, his little lungs weren't quite ready. He's having some trouble breathing.'

Ashley's mum told her that lungs are like sacks inside your chest. They fill up with air as you breathe in, a bit like balloons. Then when you breathe the air out, they deflate again. Ashley breathed in and out. In and out. She thought about the air going in through her nose.

She felt the rush of it inside her nostrils. She put her hands on her chest and imagined the two balloons inside it filling up and going down.

Normally, Ashley didn't have to think about her breathing. No one did. It was just something that happened. But the baby's wasn't happening. Not properly. Not by itself. So a special machine was being used to help him.

Ashley wanted to see her dad, but she didn't make a fuss. Rob was busy with the new baby who couldn't breathe by himself. Ashley understood that. But it didn't mean that she had to care about the baby, too. Why should she? The baby was taking up her dad's time. The baby was going to move into *her* bedroom in Holly Hill. And Ashley still couldn't work out why he was in hospital or would be in her bedroom, or anywhere. There was no reason for him to have been born at all. His dad and Cathy already had a child.

Her.

As it turned out, it wasn't until about a month later that Rob was finally able to leave Holly Hill. The baby was still in hospital, but he was breathing on his own now. The doctors had said he could go home in the next few days.

So the first thing Rob did was to climb in the car and go and collect Ashley. He was very tired from disturbed nights in hospital and all the worry about the baby.

'Are you sure you're all right to drive?' Ashley heard her mum ask Rob several times before they set off back to Holly Hill. 'If you're that tired, you should at least stop here for a couple of hours before heading back.'

'I'm fine,' Rob insisted. 'Stop making such a fuss. It's two hours away, that's all, not the other side of the world.'

Once they were off in the car together, it almost felt to Ashley as though nothing had changed. Although she knew it had, of course. 'Soon' had come round 'too soon' and now nothing would ever be the same again. But for a little while, on the drive to Holly Hill, it was just Ashley and her dad, the way it used to be.

'I'm sure you've grown since I last saw you,' Rob grinned. 'You look huge! Absolutely huge! Mind you, I've spent the last few weeks looking at a tiny baby, so that might have something to do with it.'

Ashley didn't want to talk about the baby, so she didn't reply.

'Mummy didn't tell you his name, did she?' Rob went on.

Ashley shook her head. She hadn't even thought to ask about it; hadn't wondered what it was.

'That's good,' Rob said. 'I asked her not to. I wanted to tell you myself. You see, Cathy's dad loves going fishing in Scotland, and while Cathy was growing up, sometimes she'd go with him. His favourite river is the Clyde. She says that's where she spent some of her happiest holidays. So that's what we've named the little boy. Clyde.'

Ashley was silent.

'Well?' said her dad. 'What do you think? It's a good name, isn't it? I think you're going to like having a little brother called Clyde.'

Ashley, however, was sure that she wouldn't. She could never even think of 'Clyde' as a brother. Clyde was just there. In her bedroom at her dad's house. In her life. And Ashley wished he wasn't.

Not that she said anything or made life difficult. Instead she just got on with it. As the years passed and

Ashley grew older, she worked hard at school. She was always polite. Even when her weekly visits to Holly Hill gradually turned into twice-monthly visits, she didn't make a fuss. Rob would have made the journey more often, but Cathy felt that some weekends should be just for Clyde.

Eventually, Rob did manage to get them all a bigger house. He found one on the Dixons Estate on the edge of Holly Hill. There was a third bedroom, so Ashley and Clyde didn't have to share any more. But that third room was never *Ashley's* bedroom. It was the spare room where Ashley could sleep when she stayed for the weekend. It was also the overflow room, full of the bits and pieces that didn't seem to fit anywhere else in the house. A lot of those bits and pieces were Clyde's.

'We'll get it sorted one day,' Ashley's dad was always promising, but of course, one day never came. 'One day' was like 'soon', Ashley thought. **What did it mean anyway?**

? ? ? ? ? ? ? ?

What Ashley didn't realise back then was that, in her dad's eyes, his second child, Clyde, would never match up to his first. It wasn't that Rob didn't love his son. Of course he did. But somehow he couldn't help comparing him to his daughter.

When Clyde was born, the first thing Rob found himself thinking about was the time when *Ashley* was born. He remembered seeing Ashley for the first time. He remembered holding her and hearing her cry. She was beautiful. He'd been so amazed by her tiny fingers and toes. Clyde's fingers and toes were even tinier, but when Rob looked at them, all he could see was baby Ashley's.

When Rob read stories to Clyde, he couldn't help thinking of the story times he'd shared with Ashley. When he looked over Clyde's reports (which weren't always good) from his primary school teachers, he compared them with Ashley's, which were always glowing. In fact, it seemed to Clyde that his dad was constantly grumbling at him.

Cathy sometimes asked Rob why he was always so hard on Clyde. Rob said he wouldn't have to be if Clyde wasn't so troublesome. And almost whenever Rob looked at him, all he could think was, 'The problem with you, Clyde, is … you'll never be like Ashley.'

Four

Benny flipped over on the grass and slammed down onto his back.

'Are you all right, Benny-Benns?' asked Paul.

He and Danny were trying their hardest not to laugh, but Benny looked so funny. One minute he was upside down, taking a couple of wobbly 'steps' forward as he walked on his hands. The next, his legs were flailing in the air and he toppled over backwards, hitting the ground with a loud, 'Oof!'

'Are you laughing at me?' he groaned.

'No,' spluttered Danny. 'Well … not really … Well … maybe a bit.'

That was the moment he and Paul exploded into fits of giggles, unable to hold them in any longer.

'Thanks a lot,' muttered Benny.

The Topz Hand-Walk Challenge had been all his idea. The three boys had to walk on their hands between two fixed points. In this case, the two points were Benny and Danny's bikes. They'd laid them down on the grass in the park a short distance away from each other. The winner would be the one who managed the most 'steps' between the bikes.

So far, Danny was doing the best. He'd completed five hand steps before overbalancing. Paul had found he couldn't even manage a proper handstand. Then it was Benny's turn.

'Watch and learn, Topzies!' Benny had declared.

'Watch and learn!'

Springing onto his hands, he'd scissored his legs easily into the air. But he'd only managed to totter forward a tiny way when his feet had somehow propelled him over backwards and he'd ended up flat out on the grass.

'So, what exactly are we meant to learn from that, Benny?' smirked Paul, desperately wishing he could keep a straight face.

'Oh, ha ha,' Benny scowled. He rolled over and pushed himself upright.

'Yay, he's up!' cheered Danny. 'All ready for round two?'

'Forget it,' Benny replied. 'Feet are for walking. Hands definitely aren't.'

'Then the winner of the Topz Hand-Walk Challenge is –' crowed Danny, **'ME!'**

Just to rub it in, he threw himself into a perfect cartwheel, landing neatly on his feet in front of his friend.

It was when he straightened up that he spotted the red-haired Dixons boy. He was standing by Benny's bike, staring down at it, stony-faced, as it lay on the grass.

Danny stiffened.

'What?' Benny asked. He followed his friend's gaze – and his heart sank. *Great*, he thought. *Clyde.*

How had one of the Dixons Gang managed to creep up without them noticing? Most of the time, any one of the Topz Gang could spot Dixons from a mile off. It was as if they'd developed some kind of special 'Dixons radar'. After all, the Dixons Gang were usually trouble, so Topz did everything they could to avoid them. Whenever they got in each other's way, the chances were it would turn out badly.

At least this time Clyde seemed to be on his own. There was no sign of the other two, Rick and Kevin.

Almost as soon as Danny spotted Clyde, he bent down and picked up his bike. He didn't want the Dixons boy getting his hands on it. Fortunately, it was close enough for him to grab it quickly.

Benny, on the other hand, wasn't anywhere near his. His first thought was to walk over, pick the bike up and ride off as fast as he could. But he knew Dixons. He knew that if Clyde thought he was worried about his bike, he'd be all the more likely to do something to it. Kick it, stamp on it; even grab it and ride away on it himself. In any case, if the three Topz boys cleared off now, it would look as if they were scared. And after all this *was* just Clyde on his own. Dixons often did mean things to show off in front of each other. Maybe Clyde would leave them alone as he was by himself.

Benny glanced at Paul who was standing next to him, blinking nervously. Someone needed to say something, that was obvious. They couldn't just ignore him.

So Benny cleared his throat and asked as casually as he could, 'All right, Clyde?'

For a moment, Clyde didn't reply, then, 'What's this doing here?' he muttered.

He was clearly in a bad mood.

'It's my bike,' mumbled Benny.

'I know it's your bike, idiot,' growled Clyde. 'But why is it here? On the grass? *In my way*?'

Benny's eyes flicked back to Paul, then to Danny. They could all tell where this was leading.

'Sorry,' Benny said. 'We were just leaving anyway. I'll move it.'

He took a step towards the bike, but that's what Clyde was waiting for. 'No, you won't,' he grunted. '*I'll* move it.'

Tucking a foot under the frame, Clyde jerked the bike upright. Then, with one hand on the saddle and the other on the handlebars, he gave it a shove. It shot forward towards the tarmac path leading to the park gates. Benny lunged for it to catch it if he could. But he was too slow and the other two Topz were too far away. They could only watch as the front wheel twisted inwards and the bike crashed down sideways onto the path.

Without looking back at Clyde, Benny ran to it. He grabbed it up off the ground where the back wheel was spinning crazily. From a quick glance, he could see that nothing was broken, but he was furious. Just every now and again, Dixons got to him so much that he couldn't stop himself sniping back at them.

'What is *wrong* with you?' he yelled at Clyde. 'What did you do that for?'

'Teach you a lesson, Topz boy!' Clyde shouted back. 'You shouldn't leave your cranky old bike in my way!'

'It wasn't *in* your way!' screeched Benny.

Danny took a step towards him. 'Leave it, Benny,' he said quietly. 'Come on, let's go.'

'I don't have to go,' Benny argued. 'I've got as much right to be here as he has.'

'Yeah, I know,' answered Danny. 'But sometimes it's not worth it. It's just better to be somewhere else.'

There was a pause. Then Danny added, 'Ready to go, Paul? It's youth club later anyway. We may as well get back now.'

Benny was still staring at Clyde. Clyde gazed back at him, his blue eyes cold. Weirdly, though, despite coming out on top, he didn't seem triumphant. He just looked angry.

Finally, Benny turned his bike around and began pushing it smartly towards the park gates.

'You shouldn't let it get to you, Benny,' said Danny, walking quickly to keep up. 'That's what Dixons want. You know it is.'

'Yes, I *do* know!' Benny snapped. 'But it *does* get to me, all right? It's not fair. The only reason you don't care is because it wasn't your bike.'

Danny frowned. 'That's not true. I don't like seeing you getting picked on.'

'Yeah, well, you didn't do much about it, did you?'

For a moment there was silence. Then Paul said awkwardly, 'OK, so … does anyone want to come back to my house? I think Mum was making a cake.'

Benny shook his head. 'No.' He swung his leg across his bike and hopped onto the saddle. 'I'm going home.'

Paul and Danny watched him cycle away.

'I'd like a bit of cake, thanks,' Danny said quietly.

An hour later, Clyde was still in the park. He sat on a swing, his heels resting on the ground as he rocked himself backwards and forwards. A few other children were playing on the roundabout a short distance away. They didn't go near him. Topz weren't the only ones who avoided Dixons.

Suddenly, Clyde's phone bleeped.

'Finally,' he grunted, fishing in his pocket for the mobile. It was a text from Rick: *Where r u?*

Jabbing with his thumb, he texted back: *Park.*
Where r u? Almost instantly another text from Rick bleeped in telling Clyde he'd be there soon.

Stuffing his phone away, Clyde slouched on the swing. He'd been trying to get hold of his friend for the last hour. The waiting had made him even grumpier. He couldn't text Kevin because Kevin had broken his phone. His mum had said he'd have to save up his

31

pocket money if he wanted another one. At least Rick was on his way now.

It was a late October afternoon. The daylight was just beginning to fade and it was getting colder. Clyde shivered. The children on the roundabout seemed to have left. He was on his own.

But nothing would make him go home. Not that day. Not until he absolutely had to.

Clyde's dad had given him the news a few weeks ago. The Dixons boy had been prowling around with a face like thunder ever since. But he hadn't told anyone why. Not even Rick and Kevin.

'Things are going to be a bit different round here, Clyde,' Rob had said to him after breakfast one morning. 'Not sure for how long exactly, but a couple of years at least. It's your sister. She's going to be coming to live with us.'

For a moment, the words hadn't sounded real. *Ashley? Coming to live with them?* No. That was impossible. Clyde thought he must have misunderstood.

'Her stepdad's being made redundant,' Rob went on. 'He's losing his job. But, there is an opening for him with the same company if he's prepared to move to Canada. He's up for it and Ashley's mum wants them all to go. Ashley, though, wants to stay here so she can finish school where she lives. She can't, of course, because her stepdad needs to take that job. So, the next best thing is for her to come and live here with us and go to Bruford Secondary. At least that way she'll get to finish her education in England.'

Clyde listened in disbelief. This was a joke. It had to be. How could Ashley possibly move in with them? Even when she came for a weekend, Clyde stayed out of the house as much as he could. Ashley was his dad's perfect 'other' child. The one who could never do a thing wrong. The one who always did everything better than Clyde. She learnt faster. She was so much more polite. She was popular with her teachers, popular where she lived.

Ashley was the number one child Clyde would never match up to, according to Rob, their dad. At least that's how it always seemed.

That's why Clyde hated his half-sister.

Clyde's mum, Cathy, knew how he was feeling. As Rob finished giving him the news, she stood, arms folded, watching her son. Her forehead creased into an anxious frown.

'It'll be all right, Clyde,' she said quietly. 'We'll all get along fine, you'll see.'

'We'd better,' grunted Rob. 'If we don't, I'll know exactly where the problem lies.'

'Don't say things like that, Rob,' Cathy answered, as calmly as she could. 'Why do you always have to expect the worst from Clyde?'

Rob shrugged. 'Because he never shows me his best.'

Clyde had heard enough. He leapt up from the kitchen table, thumping it with his fists.

'Yeah, well, you never give me a chance, do you?' he yelled. 'You've already decided I'll never be as good as her!'

'Clyde!' snapped Cathy. 'Don't talk to your dad like that!'

'Why not? He's allowed to talk to me however *he* wants!'

There was a moment's silence. Then Rob said grimly, 'You know what? As far as I'm concerned, my Ashley can't come here soon enough. She'll be a positive influence in this house. All I hope is that some of her good nature rubs off on you.'

As Clyde slammed the front door, he heard his mum calling after him.

'Clyde! Clyde, don't go, not like this. Let's talk about it! Clyde!'

Talk about it? Talk about what? How Ashley was about to ruin Clyde's life even more than she had done already?

Clyde ran through the front gate and out onto the pavement. He didn't stop running until the house, the street, and the Dixons Estate were far behind him.

Five

In the few moments it had taken Paul and Danny to reach the park gates after their run-in with Clyde, they'd decided not to go back to Paul's for cake. As tempting as it was, Benny was upset. The two Topz boys didn't want him to stay angry with them. They needed to sort it out.

Benny was still outside when they reached the flats where he and Danny lived. His bike was leaning against a tree. There were four small trees growing at the corners of the stretch of grass in front of the building. In spring, they were covered in blossom. Each year when the petals fell, they drifted onto the paved paths where they looked like snow.

Benny was crouching down, inspecting his bike closely.

'Is your bike all right, Benny?'

At the sound of Danny's voice, Benny glanced up.

'I think so,' he nodded. 'What are you doing here? I thought you'd both be stuffing down cake by now.'

'You were cross with us,' shrugged Paul. 'We wanted to say sorry.'

'Yeah,' said Danny. 'I didn't mean to wind you up. It's just, you can't win with Dixons. Yelling only makes things worse, you know it does. We all agreed, didn't we? If they start something, it's best just to walk away. But I'm sorry if you thought I wasn't sticking up for you. That's not what I meant.'

Benny stood up. 'Do you mean you gave up the chance of a piece of Paul's mum's cake just to come round here and say that?'

'Well … yeah,' shrugged Danny.

'Although,' said Paul, 'not exactly. I mean, the cake'll still be there. If you wanted to come round now, we could all have some.'

There was a pause, then Benny's face broke into a grin. 'So, what are we waiting for?'

Danny smiled, too.

'Anyway you don't have to be sorry,' Benny added. 'You didn't do anything. It's me, isn't it? I'm the one who got angry. It's just hard sometimes, I guess. When Dixons are nasty I can't help getting cross with them. I know I'm not supposed to, but I do. I mean, if Clyde had broken my bike, even God would have been angry with him, wouldn't He? Just a little bit?'

But even as Benny said it, he knew he was wrong.

'God does get angry,' Greg, the Sunday Club leader at church, had once told him. 'He gets angry and upset when people are unkind to each other, or unfair to each other. He doesn't like it when people are selfish, when they tell lies, when they hurt each other. But it's not *people* He gets angry with. It's the nasty things they do that He hates. The people who do them – and that's you and me sometimes, too, remember – well, He never stops loving them. And that's what He wants us to do, too – **keep on loving people no matter what they do.'**

'You've been ages!' snapped Clyde as Rick and Kevin wandered over to him where he was still sitting on a swing. 'I'm freezing out here. Where have you been?'

'What do you mean, ages?' said Rick. 'I came straight here. I only stopped to get Kevin.'

'I've been texting you for an hour,' grumbled Clyde.

'Well, I didn't know, did I?' Rick muttered. 'I was charging my phone. I've only just turned it back on.'

'Anyway, we're here now,' interrupted Kevin. 'What's so important?'

'Youth club. Tonight,' Clyde announced. 'We're going.'

'What? Why?' asked Rick.

'Yeah, boring!' said Kevin.

'It won't be boring,' insisted Clyde. 'Topz are going.'

'So?' shrugged Rick. 'They always do, don't they?'

It wasn't until Clyde had told them about his run-in with Benny in the park that the other two Dixons boys started to get interested.

'So what's the plan?' asked Kevin.

'I just want us to go and mess about,' answered Clyde. 'That Greg won't chuck us out. He never does. Benny was really wound up when he left here. I want to wind him up a bit more.'

Kevin sniggered.

'OK,' Rick nodded. 'It's not like we're doing anything else. Mum's got some party thing going on later. Clothes swapping or something. She's got all her friends coming round. I'd just as soon be somewhere else. It'll be all, "All right, Rick? How are you? Aren't you getting tall!"' He put on a high-pitched voice.

Clyde couldn't help grinning. Then his phone bleeped and the text from his mum wiped the grin clean away: *Ashley's just arrived. Where are you?*

He didn't text back. He just stuffed the phone into his pocket.

'Who was that?' asked Kevin.

'No one,' Clyde mumbled.

'So where are we meeting?' Rick wanted to know.

'What do you mean?' Clyde frowned. 'We've met. We're here.'

'Yeah, but it's an hour till youth club. I'm starving. Mum's doing lasagne. I said I wouldn't be long.'

'And since when do you care about being late home?'

Rick shook his head. 'I don't, do I? But, like I said, I'm starving.'

'Me, too,' agreed Kevin. 'Let's meet back here in a bit.'

'Why can't we get chips?' demanded Clyde.

'What's the problem with going home?'

Clyde didn't answer. His friends still didn't know that Ashley was moving in. He'd kept hoping that something would happen to stop it all. Even at the very last minute. Maybe Ashley's mum and stepdad wouldn't have to go to Canada after all. Or, if they did, perhaps Ashley would decide to go, too. But he couldn't hope any more. His mum's text had said that Ashley had arrived. Ashley was here.

In his house.

Ashley was going to be sharing his life and there was nothing Clyde could do about it.

Except not go home.

'Go and eat, then,' Clyde muttered finally. 'I'll wait for you here.'

As he watched his friends amble away, he searched his pockets for change and pulled out a small handful of coins. He might have enough for chips, but he'd get them later, after youth club. Right now, he didn't feel hungry.

Clyde pulled up his hood and headed over to the slide. He climbed the steps and sat huddled at the top. He wasn't in anyone's way. There was no one else around.

He didn't want to think about Ashley but he couldn't

stop himself. He couldn't stop the pictures that flooded through his head: his mum and dad welcoming Ashley into her new home.

'This is *your* bedroom now, Ashley.' Clyde could hear Rob saying it. 'I know it was always the spare room in the past, but now it's totally yours. I've even done it up for you. Cathy helped, didn't you, love? We just want you to feel that this is your place. Your home. Where you belong. Anything you want, all you've got to do is ask.'

Clyde clenched his teeth and his face twisted up in anger. He remembered all the visits. All those weekends when Ashley came to stay. When he was small, Ashley used to have to share Clyde's bedroom. His dad had always insisted that the room belonged to both of them, but Clyde had never felt that way. It was *his*. Ashley was always the intruder. She invaded Clyde's space and Clyde didn't want her there.

When Clyde was a bit older and his dad moved them all into a bigger house – the house they lived in now on the Dixons Estate – at least Ashley had a different room to sleep in. But Clyde liked the fact that it was still the 'spare' room. It didn't 'belong' to Ashley. There just wasn't anywhere else for her to go. It was as if Ashley was the 'spare' child. The one there wasn't a place for.

Except that to Clyde, somehow, it always felt like it was the other way round. *He* was the spare part in the family, not Ashley. *He* was the one who didn't fit. What would it be like having his half-sister there all the time? Eating together. Watching TV together.

As Clyde shuddered at the thought, he suddenly remembered something. How could he have forgotten? It had stayed in his head for weeks afterwards. On one of Ashley's visits a few years ago, Rob's camera had got broken. Ashley had been fiddling with it. Clyde had seen her. When Rob discovered it wasn't working any more, there was no question in his mind as to who the culprit was.

'Clyde!' Rob had yelled. 'How many times must I tell you not to mess about with things that don't belong to you!'

Clyde tried to defend himself, but his dad got even angrier. Both Ashley and Clyde knew who really broke the camera. But Ashley never said a word.

Clyde's phone bleeped again. Another text from his mum: *What are you playing at? Ashley's here. We're eating soon. Come home now.*

He jabbed at the keypad moodily with his thumb and deleted the message. He glanced at the time. It was 5.50pm. Rick and Kevin should be back in a minute. Then he'd have something else to think about: youth club – and how they could spoil it for the Topz Gang. Just imagining the look on Benny's face when the three of them turned up made him smile. The evening would end, of course, and then he'd have to go home, but not before he'd made himself feel heaps better.

Six

'Benny!' called Greg, 'The idea is that the ball ends up in the bucket – not in my coffee!'

Greg had organised some team games for this week's youth club. The game of the moment was to try and get a ball in a bucket after bouncing it just once on the floor. The hall was very noisy with teammates cheering each other on. When it was Benny's turn to stand behind the line, he picked the ball up confidently. He knew he'd have no trouble hitting his target. Benny had a really good eye for games like this.

But just as he'd gone to throw the ball into its bounce, he'd seen the door at the far end of the hall swing open, and the Dixons Gang walk in. Instantly, the tennis ball had flown out of his hand at an angle and knocked Greg's mug of coffee right off the snack bar. The mug smashed on the wooden floor, but Benny didn't even notice. His eyes were glued to the boys who'd just strolled in.

Greg followed his gaze. *OK*, he thought, catching sight of Dixons. As noisy as this evening's youth club was, everything was under control. But with the arrival of these three, who knew what they had in mind to make sure things didn't go to plan? Leaving the broken pieces of mug behind the snack bar to clear up later, Greg made his way towards them.

'Hello there,' he said. 'We're playing some team games. Come to join in?'

The boys sniggered.

'What would we want to do that for?' Clyde scoffed.

'Well,' replied Greg, in a cool, no-nonsense voice, 'that's what we're doing. So, if you want to join us this evening, that's what you'll be doing, too.'

For a moment, the three boys stared at him, trying to work out if he was joking.

Kevin decided he wasn't. 'I'm good at team games,' he smirked.

'Then that's a great start,' Greg said.

Clyde had spotted Benny at more or less the same instant as Benny had spotted him. He glanced at his two Dixons friends, then nodded towards the shaggy-haired Topz boy.

'I think we should join Benny's team,' he grinned. 'They look like they need all the help they can get.'

He went to step forward but Greg was ready for him.

'No, no,' he smiled. 'Sorry, boys, but that's not how it works. I'm the one that puts people into teams. In any case, we can't have three of you joining the same team. That would make the numbers too uneven. I need to split you up.'

Again Dixons stared at Greg. It was the same thing whenever they turned up at youth club. They always found it hard to work out what he was thinking. Or what he would say next. When they did things wrong at school, which happened quite often, usually a teacher would yell at them. Next minute they'd find themselves outside the head teacher's office. It didn't bother them much. They'd grown to expect it.

But Greg was different. Whatever trouble Dixons were causing, he managed to deal with it without raising his voice. Several times in the past, he'd told them he'd be praying for them. Kevin and Rick had just sniggered. But Clyde had once asked him why.

'Because God's really interested in you,' Greg had replied.

At the time Clyde had thought, *Yeah, right. Why would God be interested in me?*

Even so, every now and then, if he was feeling especially unhappy, he'd remember Greg's words.

At this particular moment, however, Greg's words were simply annoying. Clyde didn't want to be ordered about. He didn't want to be told which team he could join. The whole point of being there was to get at Benny. To do that, Clyde really needed to be on Benny's team. But he knew that, for sure, that wasn't where Greg would put him.

He was right, too.

The ball in the bucket game had come to an end. The teams were chatting among themselves, waiting for Greg to tell them what game they were going to play next. No one was very happy to see that Dixons had turned up. Topz were the unhappiest of all.

'What are they doing here?' Benny muttered to Paul.

Paul shrugged. 'Dunno,' he answered. 'Maybe it's got something to do with earlier in the park.'

'Mmm,' nodded Benny. 'That's just what I was thinking.'

'Right!' Greg's voice cut through the chatter. 'We've got another three joining us,' he announced. 'Rick, Kevin, Clyde.'

As he said each name, Greg pointed towards a different team. With one last look at each other, Dixons slouched over to join their three groups. Benny and Paul were part of the fourth team that didn't have to make room for a Dixons boy. But that didn't make Benny feel any better. He was still having to share the same airspace with them – and he didn't trust them an inch.

The next game Greg had planned involved dribbling a football. But with Dixons joining in, he could see how things could easily get out of hand.

Thinking quickly, he announced, 'That's enough of the sporty stuff, I think. Let's have a quiz.'

Quite a few children in the teams cheered. Sarah and Josie, the two girls in the Topz Gang, were especially pleased. They loved quizzes. Benny did, too, but nothing could make him enjoy himself now. With the arrival of Dixons, all the fun had gone out of the evening.

'A quiz?' grunted Rick grumpily.

Kevin and Clyde didn't look too happy, either. But Greg knew what he was doing. A question and answer session gave Dixons far less opportunity to cause havoc than if they were kicking a ball around. Even so, whenever it was Benny's turn, Clyde tried to disrupt things by shouting out stupid answers. Kevin and Rick copied, interrupting whenever any one of the Topz Gang went to speak. But the two of them soon got bored. No one around them was joining in or seemed to find what they were doing clever or funny. Eventually, Greg told them they'd all have to sit out if they carried on.

By this time, Kevin and Rick had had enough.

'Don't want to do your stupid quiz anyway,' snapped Kevin.

'Yeah, what are we here for, Clyde?' muttered Rick. 'I've got better things to do than hang around with a bunch of saddos. I'm off.'

As Clyde chased after them across the church hall, he threw Benny a vicious glance.

'Come on, don't go yet,' he frowned, once they

were all outside. 'Let's hang about and wait till they've finished. Hey! We could follow Benny home or something. Really freak him out!'

'And then what?' complained Kevin. 'What's the point? I'm going home.'

'Me, too,' agreed Rick. 'It's freezing out here.'

'What about your mum's party thing?' Clyde reminded him. 'I thought you didn't want to be at home?'

'I'd rather be there than hanging around this dump doing nothing.'

Clyde was getting desperate. Part of tonight's plan had been to get at Benny. A bigger part – a much, much bigger part – had been to stay out. He didn't want to go home. Ashley was there. Not just for a visit. She was there to stay, and Clyde didn't want to have anything to do with her. He couldn't go back to his house. Not yet. He couldn't face it.

'Well, let's do something else, then,' he said. 'We could go back to the park.'

Rick shook his head at him as if he was mad. 'It's dark, Clyde.'

'Well, let's go down to the shopping centre then. I've got a bit of money. Maybe we'd have enough to go bowling.'

Clyde knew he didn't have that sort of money. He barely had enough for chips. But he had to say something to get his friends to stay.

'How much have you got?' Kevin asked.

'Well, I – I dunno, but –'

'You haven't got any, have you?'

'I have!'

'Clyde, we're going home, all right?' said Rick. 'Just go home, too.'

He and Kevin turned to head back to the Dixons Estate. They'd barely taken a couple of steps before Clyde shouted out, 'I don't want to go home!'

Kevin swung back. 'Why not?' he demanded.

'It doesn't matter. I just don't want to go. Not yet.'

Rick's face broke into a broad grin. 'Oh, yeah? Someone's in trouble. What have you done, Clyde?'

'Nothing.'

'You must have done something. Why else wouldn't you want to go home?'

Before he could stop himself, at last Clyde blurted it out. 'Because Ashley's there! She's come to live with us.'

'What?' Kevin's eyebrows shot up. 'When did that happen?'

Kevin and Rick knew about Ashley vaguely from the times she had come to stay at Clyde's house. Every now and then, they'd see her in the park. They knew Clyde didn't like her being there, but they didn't really know why. It wasn't something they ever thought about. Except to joke that when it was an 'Ashley weekend', they could count on Clyde being in a bad mood.

'Today,' Clyde mumbled.

'Why?' Rick asked. 'I thought she lived with her mum.'

'She did. But her mum's moving to Canada with her stepdad and Ashley doesn't want to go. So she's come here.'

'What, for good?'

'I don't know. Till she finishes school I think. She's going to Bruford Secondary.'

'How old is she?'

Clyde shrugged. 'Not sure. Fourteen, maybe fifteen.'

'Well, that's all right,' said Kevin. 'She's at a different school from you. She's way older so she'll be doing different stuff. You'll hardly have to see her.'

'Of course I'll have to see her!' Clyde snapped. 'She's living in my house, Kev! How can I not see her?'

'Only trying to help,' grunted Kevin.

'You'll get used to it,' said Rick. 'At least you don't have to share a house with *my* two little sisters. They never leave me alone. They're always in my bedroom.'

Clyde threw him a look. 'Well, Ashley better stay out of my room. *Right* out of it.' He clenched his jaw and gritted his teeth together.

He was still grinding them over each other as he watched his two friends amble off back to the estate. Reaching into his pocket, Clyde pulled out the coins he knew were inside. He'd already checked, but he counted them up once more to make sure he had enough for chips. Then he turned and headed off up the road towards the shopping centre.

Seven

'What's going on, Benny?' Greg asked at the end of youth club. 'Clyde really seemed to have it in for you tonight.'

'It's not my fault,' Benny answered. 'He tried to break my bike this afternoon so I yelled at him.'

'Boy, did he yell!' nodded Paul. 'My ears are still buzzing.'

'It wasn't that bad,' frowned Benny. 'Anyway, I know what you're going to say,' he added, glancing back at Greg. 'Shouting about stuff doesn't help.'

'Huh!' Greg grinned. 'You know me so well.'

When Benny got home from youth club, the last thing he felt like doing was praying for Clyde. Why should he ask God to bless a Dixon, and be close to him? Why should he care whether or not a Dixon understood about God's love? It wasn't fair. Dixons were mean and nasty, every single one of them. They didn't deserve God's love, did they? Benny had said that to Greg not so long ago, another time when one or other of the Dixons Gang had upset him. Greg had smiled, and told him he sounded like Jonah in the Bible.

God wanted Jonah to go to a place called Nineveh and tell the people there to stop disobeying Him. If they didn't, He would have to punish them. But Jonah didn't like the people who lived in Nineveh. He *wanted* God to punish them for their bad behaviour. So he didn't do as God asked. He ran away instead. God, however, was determined that Jonah should do exactly as He'd told him to. So He arranged for him to be swallowed by a huge fish to give him time to change his mind and decide to do what God wanted after all.

'Are you saying I might get swallowed by a big fish if I don't pray for Dixons?' Benny had asked.

'Probably not,' grinned Greg. 'But if you *do* pray for them, you'll be showing God that you love them, and that's what He wants you to do.'

'But I *don't* love them,' Benny argued. 'I don't even *like* them.'

'I know. So if you pray for them, it just might help you feel differently.'

Every now and again, Benny *did* feel differently about Dixons. He wished he could tell them how much God loved them. He wished he could be their friend. But then they'd go and do some horrible thing or other – be bullies, break something, call someone names – and he'd feel angry and fed up with them all over again.

After supper, Benny went to his bedroom and sat on the floor with his back up against the end of his bed. He turned the whole scene in the park over in his mind. The picture that stayed with him the most was Clyde's face. He'd looked furious. More furious than Benny ever remembered seeing him. But there was something sad about him, too. Somewhere behind his eyes. And as much as Benny didn't want to talk to God about a Dixon, somehow, he just couldn't help it.

How can You love them, God? How can You care about Dixons? We've tried to make friends with them, but they hate Topz. Whatever we do – if we try to be nice to them or if we just ignore them – nothing's ever right. It seems like all they want to do is pick on us and make us feel bad. I don't know how Greg keeps his cool when they come to youth club. They never join in properly. The only reason they turn up at all is to make trouble. I bet they sit in the park and plan what horrible thing they're going to do next: 'What can we get away with that'll wind up Topz this time?' I can hear them saying it. 'And especially stupid Benny. Let's **really** annoy him.'

So why should I pray for them, God? Why should I care whether they ever make friends with You? They don't care how miserable they make **me**.

The trouble is, when I think about Clyde and what he did to my bike today, I just know there's something wrong. More than usual anyway. At Sunday Club, quite often Greg encourages us to pray for all the families in Holly Hill. He says it's important because there are lots of things that can make family life difficult. Sometimes families don't have enough money, so they worry all the time. Then there are parents who don't get on very well with each other. If they split up, the children have to get used to one of their parents not being there any more. And often they'll have to start living with a step-parent – a stepmum or a stepdad. But that's not all. When step-parents come along, sometimes they have children of their own already. Then suddenly there are stepbrothers and stepsisters to live with, too. Greg says it can be tough on kids. And I know it must be like that sometimes for Dixons, but why does that make them so mean? Especially to us in Topz. We'd be friends with them if only they'd let us. They just won't.

Thank You, for my family, God. I mean, Mum and Dad sometimes get in a bad mood, but then I sometimes *get in a bad mood, too. I'm in one now, if you hadn't noticed. And I know Mum wishes we were living in a house with a garden rather than our flat, but we're happy most of the time. Usually we all get on really well. I don't know if Dixons are ever happy. When I see them mucking about together, they seem all right, except ... I don't know ... it's as if deep down inside themselves, they're always angry about something.*

*I know Clyde was angry today, God. It wasn't just inside him, it was all over his face. I don't think I've ever seen him look quite like that. I didn't care, though. It didn't stop me getting angry back. I mean, I was right to be angry, wasn't I? He shouldn't have done that to my bike. I'd never have done that to **his** bike. In fact, I'd never have touched anything of his.*

*But then, I think something really **was** wrong today. Maybe it is Clyde's family, or maybe it's nothing to do with that. Maybe it was just a full-on, Clyde-style bad mood: 'Yeah! There's Benny, I'm gonna try to break his bike!' Only somehow, I don't think so. There was something else.*

And I've got this problem, God. There's a part of me that couldn't care less and I'm sorry. I'm sorry for the part that doesn't care. Help me to care. Not just today because something's happened, but every day. And please will You bless Clyde, God? Even though he's feeling so angry, please would You somehow do something to help him?

And help me to forgive him, too.

Whatever they might do to us, Dixons are still really special to You. I know that. Please help Clyde to know it.

There was a bench outside the pasty shop in the shopping centre. Clyde sat on it after he'd left youth club, eating his chips. He didn't think he was hungry when he bought them, but as he began to tuck in, he found he was ravenous. He hadn't eaten for hours. He'd had breakfast before leaving his house, but then he'd stayed out all day. He'd passed the time wandering between the shopping centre and the park until he and the other two Dixons had paid youth club a visit. There were last minute preparations going on at home ready to welcome Ashley. Clyde didn't want to have anything to do with them.

As he shoved the last chip in his mouth, he knew he could easily eat the same portion all over again – twice. But he had no more money. He ran his tongue over his teeth and his lips. He wanted to savour the last tang of salt and vinegar.

Suddenly, the phone in his pocket rang. He didn't answer it. He knew who it would be. His mum. She'd still be wondering where he was. She must be worried. Clyde often stayed out for hours at a time, but he always turned up when he was hungry. He'd certainly never disappeared all day before. His mum had been texting him madly, too, but Clyde had stopped reading the messages.

Cathy knew why he'd gone. She knew exactly how her son felt about having Ashley to live with them. She understood, too. She didn't like the way Rob seemed to favour his daughter so much, either.

At the same time, she realised that he felt guilty. Rob felt *so* guilty that he'd moved away from Ashley; that he hadn't been there all the time to see his little girl growing up.

Still, making Ashley into the golden child all the time to help himself feel better didn't help Clyde. Not one little bit. Nor was it entirely fair.

Cathy understood all this. She knew why she hadn't seen Clyde all day. But what she wanted right at that moment was for him just to come home. The longer he stayed out, the deeper trouble he was getting into with his dad.

Clyde screwed the paper and the little polystyrene tray that had held his chips. As he did so, his phone rang again. He gripped the bundle of rubbish so tightly that his knuckles went white. Then he sighed gloomily and dropped it into the litterbin next to the bench.

The voice behind him made him jump.

'I think someone's trying to get hold of you.'

Twisting round, Clyde found himself face to face with Greg. He'd sat down at the other end of the bench so gently that Clyde hadn't even felt the seat move.

'Hello,' Greg smiled. 'Fancy meeting you here.'

Clyde was good at smart responses. He usually had an answer to everything. But he was so taken aback to see Greg sitting next to him that, for once, he couldn't think of a thing to say.

'Sorry, didn't mean to startle you,' said Greg. 'Wouldn't have spotted you if I hadn't heard your phone ringing.'

'What do you want?' Clyde managed to grunt at last.

'Chips since you ask,' replied Greg cheerfully. 'Got to the end of youth club and thought, I'm starving!'

Clyde shook his head. 'Well, I haven't got any left. I've eaten them.'

'No, I wouldn't ask you for yours,' Greg laughed. 'I meant I've just come out to buy some.'

'Right.'

'Tell you what, though,' Greg went on, 'it's getting a bit late for you to be hanging about here on your own, isn't it?'

'No!' frowned Clyde. 'I do what I want. Anyway, I was going home in a bit.'

'Well, if you like, when I've got my chips I'll walk that way with you. We could share them. I'm sure you've got room for a few more. Do you like salt and vinegar?'

'Why would I want to go with you?' Clyde snapped. 'I'm fine on my own.'

Greg got to his feet. 'Just wondered, that's all. Up to you, though. See you around then, Clyde. Maybe you'll pop into youth club again.'

Clyde watched as Greg walked away in the direction of the chip shop. There was a part of the Dixons boy – just a very tiny part – that would have loved to walk home with Greg. It wasn't to do with getting more chips, although that would have been a bonus. It was something about the youth leader. Clyde could never quite work out what it was. Greg was just kind. He cared. Whatever he said, he really meant.

Even though Dixons had marched into youth club that evening meaning to make trouble, here was Greg offering him chips.

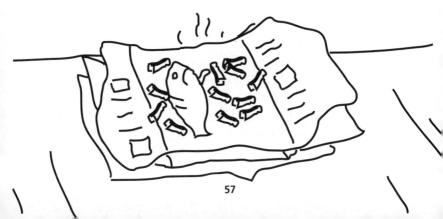

Eight

It was dark.

Clyde stood in the pool of orangey light from the streetlamp outside his house. He stared at the lounge window. He knew that behind it, in that room, they would all be gathered – his mum, his dad. And Ashley. This was the only window that glowed with a warm light behind the drawn curtains. The rest of the house looked to be in darkness.

He shivered. He felt as if he'd been cold forever. But as cold as he was, Clyde didn't want to go indoors. He'd been dreading this moment. The moment of having to go home; having to step into a new way of life that he hated before it had even begun.

The trouble was it was late. The day had worn itself out and there was nowhere else he *could* go.

He stuffed a hand into his pocket and pulled out his phone. The screen told him he'd got six new text messages and four missed calls. He opened the inbox. All six messages were from his mum. He'd known they would be. He flicked through them quickly. Each one was begging him to come home.

How different Clyde would have felt if just one of those messages had been from his dad: *Come home, son. Things are all going to turn out fine. I'll make sure of it.*

How different the whole of Clyde's life might have been if he'd only felt valued. Special. That's what it was about Greg, Clyde thought. Greg hardly knew him, and what he *did* know wasn't good. The Dixons were well known as troublemakers in Holly Hill. But when

Greg spoke to him, just for a brief moment, he did feel valued. He did feel worth something.

Well, almost.

Suddenly the lounge curtains were pulled slightly apart and Clyde saw his mum's face, peering anxiously out into the night. She spotted her son instantly. For a moment they just looked at each other. Then she raised a hand and beckoned to him.

Cathy had the front door open before Clyde reached it.

In a low voice, she mumbled quickly, 'Your dad's furious, Clyde. I've done my best, but he's going to have words, I know he is. Where have you been? Why didn't you just come back for supper like I asked you to? Why didn't you answer your phone?'

That's when Clyde's dad appeared in the hall behind her.

'Well, well, well,' he said. Clyde could hear the anger in his voice. 'So here you are at last. Come back because you're hungry, I suppose. Well, you needn't think you're getting any supper. Not after the way you've behaved. Ashley got here hours ago and where were you? Why weren't you here to help us give her a welcome? I knew you were selfish and rude but I never expected this. I'm ashamed of you, Clyde. Never mind that your mum's been worried sick. It shows no respect for your sister.'

Clyde could feel his own anger boiling up in his stomach. 'What sister?' he growled. 'I don't have a sister!'

His dad gaped at him.

'It's all right, Rob,' Cathy said. 'I'll deal with him. I'll sort it out.'

Rob ignored her. 'Get up to your room, Clyde. Right now. And in the morning, we're all going to sit down to breakfast together, as a family – your mum, me, you and Ashley. Do I make myself clear?'

For one more moment, Clyde stood there, looking into his dad's furious face. Then he pushed past his parents and stalked off upstairs. As he went, he heard another voice. It was Ashley's. She must have been standing in the lounge doorway, listening.

'I didn't mean to cause trouble, Dad. Don't be cross with Clyde. We've all got to get used to this, haven't we?'

Clyde paused at the top of the stairs. Hearing Ashley speak almost made him wince. How was he ever going to be able to live with this?

At the same time, what choice did he have?

He threw open his bedroom door and stared inside. The curtains were still open. In the harsh half-light from the street lamp outside the window, the furniture was just a series of dark, shadowy shapes. There was a stack of plastic boxes against one wall, too. They'd only been there for a few weeks, stuffed with the things of Clyde's that had been stored in the spare room. Mostly books and old toys. Clyde had quite a collection of miniature cars and motorbikes. Of course they'd all had to be squeezed into his room now that the third bedroom was for Ashley.

Clyde swung round. No one had followed him upstairs. He could still hear the sound of voices from the lounge, but they weren't loud enough for him to make out what was being said.

All of a sudden, he was filled with an urge to peep inside the spare room. To see how it looked now that Ashley had actually moved into it.

Clyde tiptoed across the landing towards the bedroom and, with one foot, pushed open the door. Flicking on the light, he gazed around. It felt to him as if the space had been invaded; invaded by Ashley's belongings.

The wardrobe door was slightly open. Some sort of denim was sticking out. Jeans possibly, or perhaps the sleeve of a jacket. There were books on the new bookshelves that Rob had put up himself last weekend. Clyde noticed one particularly fat one. He tilted his head slightly to read that it was an encyclopaedia of Formula One car racing. His dad often talked about how much his daughter liked cars. A pair of black leather, high-heeled boots and some trainers had been placed neatly in front of the wardrobe on the new carpet. They were clean and new-looking, too. The pine chest of drawers in the corner was also new.

Glancing over his shoulder to make sure no one was coming, Clyde stepped inside the bedroom. He pulled open the top drawer in the chest. It was full of t-shirts. The next one down held several jumpers and a scarf. He spotted a scarf on the bed, too. It was dark blue with a few paler blue stripes running down its length and clusters of shiny, purple sequins. Beside it lay a pair of thickly padded, blue gloves. Clyde picked one up and slipped a hand inside. He scrunched his fingers into a fist. The glove was a little too big for him but it felt soft and comfortable. Clyde didn't have any gloves. Not at the moment. As fast as his mum bought pairs for him, he lost them.

He tore the glove off and threw it back down on the bed. It was the same spare room bed, but Clyde had got home from school one day just in time to see the new mattress being delivered.

Then he spotted it. A laptop computer on the little desk under the window. Clyde could hardly believe his eyes. Was there anything this girl didn't have? Rob had kitted the room out with new stuff, and Ashley had her own laptop, too! What did Clyde have that was new in *his* room? It hadn't been touched for years, apart from a new chair. The leg on the old one had worked loose and his mum was afraid that one day it would collapse under him. Clyde's room was a dump compared to this one, he thought.

He leaned over the desk to have a closer look at the laptop.

'Open it up, if you want.'

Clyde spun round. Ashley had crept up the stairs so quietly that Clyde hadn't noticed she was standing in the bedroom doorway, watching him.

'Open it up,' Ashley repeated. 'It's a good one. My stepdad got it for me because he's disappearing off to Canada with my mum. I think it was his way of saying, "Sorry to have to leave you behind, but we're going anyway."'

Clyde stared at her. She looked different to when he'd last seen her. Her blonde hair had been long and curly but she'd had it all cut off. Now it hugged her head in a close crop. It made her look hard. Cold, almost.

Without a word, Clyde went to shove past her out of the room. But Ashley didn't move, which surprised him. Nearly five years older than her half-brother, she was that much taller, too. Clyde had to tilt his head up a little to look into her face. Ashley was gazing down at him. She didn't blink. Her expression was quite blank.

'Listen, Clyde,' she murmured. 'I don't want to be here any more than you want me here. But it looks like we're stuck with it. So let's just deal with it, yeah? And don't even think about making problems for me, because if there's any trouble – any trouble at all – I reckon we both know whose side Dad's going to be on. **Don't we?'**

A deep frown wrinkled Clyde's forehead. Had he heard that right? It was almost as if Ashley was threatening him. He didn't know how to answer, but so what? He had no intention of speaking to his half-sister anyway. However long Ashley ended up living with them, Clyde had decided he'd never say a word to her.

Turning his shoulder towards the doorway, he shoved into Ashley. But this time she didn't stop him leaving and stood back to let him by. Clyde reached his bedroom, stepped inside and slammed the door shut hard behind him.

Almost instantly, Rob's voice called up the stairs, 'Everything all right, Ashley?'

'Everything's fine, Dad,' Ashley called back, a smug grin spreading across her face. **'Just making myself at home.'**

Nine

The family breakfast Rob had planned for Ashley's first morning in her new home didn't happen. Clyde's seat at the table was empty and when Cathy wasn't talking, there were awkward silences.

Finally, Cathy reached for her phone. 'I'll just text him,' she muttered uncomfortably. 'Find out where he's got to this time.'

'What's the point?' Rob grunted. 'He won't answer, you know he won't.'

Cathy sighed and slid the phone back into her pocket.

'It doesn't matter, Dad,' Ashley said gently, smoothing a hand across her hair. 'Honestly, it doesn't. I don't want Clyde to get into trouble again.'

His dad looked at her. He smiled, reached out and put a hand on his daughter's shoulder.

'One thing's for sure,' Rob said. 'Clyde most certainly doesn't deserve a sister like you.'

Oddly enough, that was Clyde's first thought, too, when he woke up early that morning. He didn't deserve her. He didn't deserve to have his life ruined by a half-sister who shouldn't be in his house; who shouldn't be just down the landing, sleeping in the spare room.

She was his enemy.

Clyde hated Ashley. When she came to visit for weekends, Clyde had always made sure she knew that. But it had never occurred to him that Ashley hated him, too. That was as big and nasty a surprise as hearing the news that she was coming to live with them. Not that Clyde cared whether Ashley liked him or not. It just made him that much more wary. What was this girl *really* like?

After all, she was as nice as pie to Clyde in front of their dad.

But last night in her bedroom doorway, Ashley hadn't been 'nice' at all.

Clyde got up the moment he was awake. He wanted to have time to sneak out of the house before anyone else was up. Before his dad's 'family' breakfast could even be laid out on the table.

At just before seven o'clock in the morning, Clyde was dressed and downstairs in the kitchen. He was hungry, so he grabbed a couple of wrapped chocolate biscuits and a bag of crisps from the cupboard.

Then he was outside; through the front gate and off down the road. He'd go to the shopping centre. That was his plan. He could wander round looking in shop windows for a bit, then head for the park. In any case, he only needed to kill time for an hour or so. After that, Rick would be up. Clyde could text him and get him and Kevin to come out and meet him.

Clyde couldn't think much further than the next hour. Somehow or other, he had another whole day's worth of hours to get through before going home. He didn't know how he was going to fill them. He just knew that he couldn't *bear* to be in the house with Ashley there. He had to stay out.

It was the last weekend of half term. School started again on Monday. Thankfully, as Ashley was older, she'd be going to Bruford Secondary, whereas Clyde was still at Southlands Primary.

Southlands was a new school. It had only been built a couple of years ago. Until then, Clyde and the other two Dixons boys had gone to Holly Hill School, where the Topz Gang went. But all three of them had moved to

Southlands when it opened because it was closer to the Dixons Estate.

Clyde didn't like school one bit. For once in his life, though, he couldn't wait for term to start again. On school days it would be so much easier to avoid Ashley.

The shopping centre was quiet. It was early Saturday morning, so there was no rush of people trying to get to work. The only shop that was open was the bakery. Clyde glanced at the loaves and buns and cakes on display in the window. They looked good and the freshly baked smell drifting through the open doorway was even better. He reached in his pocket for one of the chocolate biscuits, pulled the wrapper off and took such a big bite that he was barely able to chew.

It was while his mouth was completely crammed that he suddenly found himself face to face with Greg. He'd just stepped out of the baker's clutching a paper bag. Clyde choked in surprise and a spray of chocolately crumbs shot into the air.

Greg frowned. 'Are you all right, Clyde?'

Clyde nodded. His face was bright red and his eyes were watering, but after a moment, he managed to recover himself.

'We must stop meeting like this,' Greg said once Clyde had stopped spluttering. 'You've caught me buying naughty food again. Last night chips, this morning iced buns. I know what you're thinking,' he went on. 'How does he keep his trim figure on a diet like that? Well, truth is I'm normally pretty healthy. I eat a *lot* of muesli. It's just that some Saturdays, I simply can't resist the lure of an iced bun.'

Clyde had finally managed to swallow the remains of

his biscuit and was wiping his mouth with the back of his hand.

'In fact,' Greg added, 'I've been a bit of a pig today. I've actually got two iced buns in here.' He shook the paper bag. 'I don't suppose you fancy one? You'd be doing me a big favour if you did.' He patted his stomach with the flat of his hand. 'I may look trim but under this big jumper, I'm actually a bit of a blubber-belly.'

Big jumper or not, to Clyde Greg looked nothing like a blubber-belly. At the same time, he knew that's not why Greg was offering him a bun. Greg was just being kind because – for some reason that Clyde could never work out – that's the way Greg was.

Finally, Clyde mumbled, 'It's all right, I've got another biscuit.'

Greg opened the bag and held it out to him. 'Oh, go on,' he said. 'Please?'

After another moment's hesitation, Clyde gave in. The iced buns looked too tasty to turn down again. Besides, he hadn't eaten a proper breakfast, so he was hungry. 'Thanks,' he muttered, pulling one out of the bag.

'Well,' smiled Greg, 'I think I might eat mine here.' He nodded towards the bench outside the pasty shop. 'Would you like to join me?'

Normally Clyde would have laughed scornfully: 'No! Leave me alone. I'm not one of your Topz Gang.'

But today didn't feel like a normal day. He had time to kill. Today he didn't know what he was going to do with himself from morning till night. More importantly, just at that moment he was on his own. The other two Dixons were probably still curled up in their beds. They weren't likely to come strolling by and see him tucking into an iced bun with Greg. So, why not spend a few minutes with him? After all, much as he hated Topz and all the God 'stuff' they did and talked about, he'd never felt that way about Greg. Somewhere inside himself, Clyde knew he even quite liked him.

They sat down together and started munching.

'So, Clyde,' Greg asked between mouthfuls, 'how's life?'

Clyde shot Greg a look. He didn't mind sitting there

but he didn't want to answer questions. He shrugged and returned to eating his bun.

'It's just that,' Greg continued, 'you're out very early for a Saturday morning, and it was pretty late when I saw you here last night. **Is everything OK?'**

Again, Clyde said nothing.

Greg smiled faintly. 'When I was your age, I wasn't much of a talker either. That comes as a bit of a surprise to people who know me now, seeing as these days it's hard to get me to shut up. But, I was actually very shy when I was a kid. Again, bit of a shocker! I used to bottle things up. I wouldn't talk to anyone about anything. But, what I found in the end,' he said gently, 'is that *not* talking about things was actually a big mistake. It just made me angrier and more upset. Then, once I started opening up to people – not just anyone, but special people who I could trust and who I knew would listen to me and try to help – things got a whole lot better.'

Clyde gave Greg another sideways look. It was hard to imagine the youth leader ever being upset over anything, and even harder to picture him being angry.

'So that's why,' Greg finished, scrunching up the paper bun bag and dabbing it across his sugary lips, 'these days I never shut up. Who could you talk to, Clyde? If you had a problem you needed help with, who could you go to?'

Clyde felt awkward. Uncomfortable. He knew he didn't have to listen to Greg any more. He could get up and walk away any time he felt like it.

But he didn't want to. Clyde never felt happy. Not really happy, not deep down. And since he'd known that Ashley was coming to live with them, he'd felt worse. He was upset every day. He felt empty; lonely. Like an outcast in his own home somehow. Now that Ashley was here and the nightmare had come true, he felt more alone than ever. But in an odd sort of way, sitting beside Greg early that morning was making him feel better.

'Who did *you* talk to?' Clyde asked at last.

'We're not talking about me, are we?' Greg replied. He waited. Clyde didn't answer.

'Tell you what,' Greg said brightly, 'I'll tell you who I talk to *most* these days, if you like.'

'Who?' Clyde grunted.

'You see, I'm fortunate because I do have some very good friends to chat with. Then, there's this one Friend who I talk to all the time. I'm always bending His ear about this and that. And He's always helping me out. I could introduce you to Him. He'd like that, I know He would. You might find it helpful to talk to Him, too.'

Clyde could feel the stickiness of the bun on his fingers. He looked at them and rubbed them together to try to clean them off.

'Yes, but who is it?' he asked.

'Might come as a surprise,' Greg answered. Then he looked Clyde full in the face as he said: 'God.'

Ten

Clyde was deep in thought when Rick and Kevin turned up in the park later that morning. So deep that he only realised they were there when Kevin bounced a football on his head.

'Oi!' Clyde shouted. 'What did you do that for?'

'We've been calling you from way over there,' retorted Kevin. 'We thought you were asleep.'

'Of course I'm not asleep,' Clyde growled. 'I just didn't see you, that's all.'

In the end, he hadn't bothered texting Rick. He knew the other two Dixons boys would turn up in the park sooner or later. After talking to Greg, he wanted to be on his own for a while. He didn't often feel that way. Most days, Clyde didn't especially like his own company. It's just that what Greg had said to him as they'd sat together on the bench outside the pasty shop had made him thoughtful.

Then again, perhaps it wasn't just *what* he had said. Perhaps it was more the way he'd said it. Clyde could see that God meant everything to Greg.

He stood up from where he'd been sitting cross-legged on the damp grass, and stretched. He felt stiff and cold.

'What time is it?' he asked.

Kevin glanced at his watch. 'Ten.'

'*Ten*?' Clyde was astonished. 'How did it get to be ten o'clock already?'

'It's this thing called "time", Clyde,' Rick replied sarcastically. 'It moves on. Don't you know anything?'

Clyde raised his eyes at him. Still, he couldn't believe

how quickly the hours had shot by since he'd gone out first thing. He knew he was in big trouble, too. The 'family breakfast' his dad had planned would have been and gone, and his seat would have been empty. His parents would have discovered he wasn't anywhere in the house. Not that they'd go looking for him. They never did that. If he switched his phone on, Clyde knew he'd probably find a string of 'where are you?' texts from his mum. But there'd be nothing from his dad, Clyde was sure of it.

'So what are we doing?' asked Kevin.

Clyde saw that he had his skateboard with him. He shrugged. Then, 'Target practice?' he suggested.

The three boys ran into the skateboard park. It was empty, which made their game easier.

Target practice involved one of them trying to skate up and down the ramps without being hit by the football, which the other two would take it in turns to kick. Kevin was by far the best kicker. His aim and timing were brilliant. He knew it, too. Dixons didn't play the game very often because it generally ended with Kevin crowing his head off and Rick and Clyde feeling disgruntled. But they always got over it, and each time they played again, they both believed that *this* would be the time they'd deliver the master kick that would send Kevin flying.

Kevin went on the skateboard first. As he scooted down the long ramp, Rick shot the ball towards him hard. It just about skimmed the back of Kevin's shoulders, but in the game, that didn't count as a hit.

'Woohoo!' shrieked Clyde. 'Close, or what! My turn.'

'No, not yet,' answered Rick. 'I'm just warming up.'

Once more, Kevin sped down the ramp. This time,

Rick tried aiming the football slightly in front of him so that he'd skate right into it. He misjudged it, though, and the ball flew over Rick's head.

'Rubbish, Rick!' said Clyde. 'You're still freezing cold.'

'One more go,' retorted Rick. 'I'll get him this time.'

'Bet you don't!' Kevin called over.

'No, give me the ball, Rick. I'll do it,' insisted Clyde.

'In a minute,' replied Rick. 'Just wait.'

Clyde never got his turn. Kevin shot down the long ramp and Rick kicked the ball at him as his friend began to bowl up the shorter one. The ball never even got close. Flying off to the left, it sailed over the fence right out of the skateboard park. Clyde went to chase after it, but then he stopped dead.

Someone had already caught it.

Ashley.

'Can I have a go?'

The girl was standing there, watching Dixons closely with her keen, greenish-brown eyes. Clyde stared back at her, his own pale blue eyes glinting with fury under his mass of red hair.

What was Ashley doing here? How dare she just turn up in the park? This was Clyde's space. He was staying out of the house to get *away* from his half-sister. What did she think she was doing following him here?

Rick, and then Kevin as he skidded the skateboard to a halt, followed Clyde's gaze. They hardly ever saw Ashley. Just once in a while when she came to stay in Holly Hill for the odd weekend. But they both recognised her instantly, despite her new haircut.

As no one answered her question, Ashley asked another one. 'Whose ball?'

'Erm … it's mine,' Rick mumbled.

'Do you mind if I have a go?'

Rick glanced towards Kevin, who shrugged, 'Fine by me.'

Clyde glared at them.

'Well, it's not like you two can ever hit me, is it?' said Kevin. 'May as well give her a go.'

Ashley strolled into the skateboard park and put the ball down. Kevin got ready at the top of the ramp. He eyed her a little scornfully. She was tall and athletic-looking, but she was still just a girl. He didn't imagine she was very strong. She probably wouldn't even be able to kick straight.

All this ran through Kevin's mind as he pushed off. He'd barely begun to scoot down the ramp before Ashley had drawn back her right foot and punched the ball with it hard. Kevin hadn't even reached the ground when it slammed into his arm just below his shoulder.

'Yesss!' yelled Rick, leaping in the air and tossing his head so that his long hair flopped in all directions. 'We've been trying to do that forever! Nice one, Ashley!'

Although he'd got whacked, even Kevin seemed impressed. He skated over to the girl with a big grin all over his face.

'Where d'you learn to kick like that?' he beamed.

'We had a girls' football team at school where I used to live,' Ashley answered. 'You had to be good to get in it. They really worked you, too. Two after school practices a week sometimes, and Saturday mornings. Plus ...' She hesitated and her eyes slid towards Clyde. 'Plus Dad used to play football with me a bit when I was a kid. Took me to some big matches, too. I've seen Manchester United play lots of times.'

Clyde was leaning up against the fence, arms folded, shoulders hunched. He kept his eyes glued to his feet. He couldn't bear so much as to look at Ashley. At the mention of his dad, the scowl on his face deepened. Had she said that on purpose? Was she trying to rub Clyde's face in the fact that she was by far the favourite? As if Clyde didn't know that already.

'So who wants to take a pop at me on the skateboard, then?' Ashley said it as if she was throwing down a challenge. 'Clyde?'

Clyde didn't twitch a muscle. He'd decided he wasn't going to talk to his half-sister before she'd even moved into his house. He certainly wasn't going to change his mind about that now.

'I'll have a go,' said Kevin.

'Cool,' Ashley answered.

'You'd better watch yourself, Ashley,' remarked Rick. 'Kevin doesn't often miss.'

'Yeah, well,' Ashley smiled, 'there's always a first time.'

Kevin didn't miss. He launched the ball into the air and watched as it bounced off Ashley's hip with a satisfying 'thwack'. Punching the air with his fists, Kevin ran around the skateboard park, yelling at the top of his voice.

'Bit over the top, Kev,' Rick said.

'Not at all. He did well,' smiled Ashley.

But there wasn't any warmth in her smile. Clyde glanced at her just long enough to see that all Ashley really looked was smug.

'Uh-oh,' Rick said suddenly. 'Look who's here.'

Ashley turned. Two boys and two girls had wandered in through the park gates. The boy was holding a small dog on a lead.

'Who's that?' she asked.

'That,' answered Kevin, 'is Topz. Four of them anyway. If there's anyone you should steer clear of in Holly Hill, it's the Topz Gang.'

Ashley raised her eyebrows. 'Scary, are they?'

'Hardly,' Rick spluttered. 'They're a pain, more like it.'

'I think I've heard Clyde mention Topz before,' Ashley nodded. 'You don't like them either, do you, Clyde?'

Clyde still wasn't talking.

Once more, a cold smile crossed Ashley's lips. 'So, if all you Dixons don't like Topz,' she continued, 'why are you letting them just stroll into your park?'

Kevin frowned. 'It's not *our* park, is it? We don't want them coming here, but we can't actually stop them.'

Ashley looked doubtful. 'Maybe you're just not trying hard enough.' She paused for a moment. Then, 'Do you want me to get rid of them?' she asked.

Rick and Kevin exchanged a look. 'Well … 'course,' muttered Kevin.

'OK,' said Ashley. 'I'll sort them out. For now, at least. I mean they obviously bother my little brother a whole lot, and if Clyde doesn't like something, I want to help fix it.'

Clyde couldn't make it out. First, Ashley had shoved her way into their game of target practice. Now she was trying to make herself sound like some saintly big sister who'd do anything to help out her 'family'. And from the admiring looks on Rick and Kevin's faces, they were falling for it.

He wanted to shout at Ashley to get lost; to tell her she had no business being in the park, and that Dixons and Topz were nothing to do with her. But at the same time, he couldn't help admiring the way she seemed so calm and in control. Other kids were nervous around Dixons. Even some of the older ones. But Ashley didn't seem phased at all.

'So what are you going to do?' Rick asked. 'How are you going to get rid of them?'

Ashley chuckled. 'Watch!'

Slipping out of the skateboard park, she crossed quickly to the main path. Then she began to run as fast as she could towards John, Benny, Sarah and Josie. John was about to let his dog, Gruff, off his lead.

When they saw the tall, lanky girl racing towards them, they all stepped sideways to get out of her way. But she came to a sudden stop in front of them.

Breathing heavily, and with a worried look on her face, Ashley puffed, 'You've got to get out of here now!'

Topz looked confused. 'What?' frowned Benny. 'What do you mean? Why?'

'Dogs aren't allowed in the park any more!' Ashley said, pointing to Gruff and still pretending to gasp for breath. 'I just saw this old man with a Labrador get fined £250. He was practically crying.'

Benny had never seen Ashley before. Neither had the other three Topz. Their first thought was that this must be a wind-up. But why would someone they didn't know want them to get out of the park?

John looked all around. 'When did this happen? There are no signs.'

'Only today,' Ashley went on. 'The signs haven't been put up yet. But the man said there was a big thing about it in the local paper.' She flung a glance over her shoulder. There were people scattered everywhere. None of them seemed to have dogs with them.

Then, 'Look, there's the warden!' Ashley cried.

'Where?' asked Josie, squinting into the distance.

'There! Right there!' yelled Ashley. 'He's seen you with your dog! Honestly, if you don't want to get a fine, you've just got to go!'

The anxiety in Ashley's face and the panic in her voice were somehow catching.

'Come on,' said John. 'I can't get a £250 fine. Dad'll go mad!'

'Yeah, you're right,' added Sarah. 'Let's get out of here.'

The four of them made their way quickly back out through the park gates with Gruff. The little dog looked less than happy at having his walk cut short. They were in such a hurry that they didn't notice Dixons in the skateboard area. Rick and Kevin were doubled up with laughter. Clyde still stood on his own, staring at Ashley in disbelief.

Ashley kept up her worried face until Topz were out of sight. Then she turned towards the skateboard park, grinned and bowed low to her Dixons audience. She was pleased with herself. She'd set out to impress Rick and Kevin and that's exactly what she'd done. And as her eyes flicked towards Clyde, Ashley could see that she'd made quite an impression on her younger half-brother, too.

Eleven

There was something about Ashley that was extremely cool. At least there was to Rick and Kevin. She was older for a start, so hanging around with her – and being seen with her – made them feel much more grown up. It didn't matter that she was a girl. She oozed confidence and had a wicked sense of humour. And she kicked a football like a champion. Rick and Kevin couldn't shut up about the way she'd seen off Topz from the park.

'I wish I had a sister like yours,' Rick said to Clyde when they were back at school after half term. 'I'm stuck with two whingey little things.'

'Yeah, Ashley's awesome!' agreed Kevin. 'I don't know why you've got a problem with her.'

The last week or so had continued to be confusing for Clyde. After that first uncomfortable moment on the night Ashley had arrived and caught Clyde in her bedroom, she seemed completely different towards him. *And* she somehow managed to keep the peace between Clyde and their dad. Clyde's mum was astonished. She was delighted, too. Ashley kept telling Clyde what a great kid he was. She even told him she was proud of her 'little brother'. Proud of the way he stood up for himself and wasn't afraid to say what he thought or show how he felt.

Ever since Ashley was a small child whose reading and writing were way ahead of the others in her class at school, her dad had remarked, 'She's got a way with words has my Ashley.' And much as Clyde didn't want to admit it, it was true. Ashley seemed to be able to talk her way round anything and anyone to get what she wanted.

She could make you feel special. Like one of a kind. Somehow she could even persuade you to think and feel the way she did.

The more time Clyde spent around his big sister, the better he began to feel about himself. And as for his vow never to speak to her, he was beginning to find more and more that he actually *wanted* to.

After a few weeks of being in Holly Hill, Ashley began to meet Clyde after school. She had to walk right past the gates to Southlands Primary to get back to the Dixons Estate from Bruford Secondary. The schools were practically next door to each other. She'd wait outside for her half-brother at the end of the day and they'd walk home together. The other two Dixons usually tagged along. Rick and Kevin loved hanging around Ashley, and Ashley seemed to like being one of the Gang. She didn't seem bothered about making friends of her own age either – or being seen with kids who were so much younger.

One day after school, as they were taking their usual short-cut along the alley behind Makepiece Avenue, they saw a man walking towards them.

'Oh, no!' groaned Kevin. 'Look who it is.'

Ashley shrugged. 'Never seen him before. Who is he?'

'It's Greg,' Rick sniggered. 'He works at the church. He's such an idiot.'

Clyde hadn't seen Greg since the day they'd shared iced buns at the shopping centre. But he'd thought a lot about what Greg had said – that it was better to talk about things that were bothering you than try to keep them to yourself. He'd thought about God being Greg's Friend, too, and always having time to listen to him. Clyde needed a friend like that. Perhaps that was why, in the end, he'd allowed himself to start getting close to Ashley.

'Greg's not an idiot,' Clyde said. The words were out of his mouth before he could stop them. Greg had been kind to him that day at the end of half term and he didn't want Rick calling him names.

Rick looked at him, astonished. **'What?'**

'He's just not an idiot, that's all.'

They were almost level with the youth leader now. He stood to one side of the alley to make room for them.

'Hello, you lot,' he smiled. 'Another hard day at school done?'

Kevin and Rick exchanged glances. Why was this man even talking to them?

'You all right, Clyde?' Greg began again. 'How's everything going?'

Clyde felt instantly awkward. He didn't want to talk to Greg in front of Dixons, but he didn't want to ignore him either. So he decided on a shrug and a 'good, yeah'.

'Great,' smiled Greg. 'See you around, then. Youth club's on later if you want to give it another go.'

As he walked away, Rick and Kevin burst into giggles.

'Sssh!' hissed Clyde. 'He'll hear you.'

'What d'you care if he does?' spluttered Kevin.

Ashley was watching Clyde carefully. 'What's going on?' she asked. 'You've gone bright red.'

Clyde had felt his face flushing the moment Greg had spoken to him.

'I'm hot,' he muttered. 'I'm just hot.'

'No, you're not,' Ashley persisted. 'You're embarrassed. Is that man a friend of yours?'

'Of course not!' Clyde tried to make a joke of it. 'He's about 104 for a start!'

At that, Rick and Kevin smirked, but not Ashley. She just fixed Clyde with her sparkling, greenish-brown eyes for a moment more, then turned and headed off out of the alley.

104

When Clyde went up to his room later that evening, Ashley came and knocked at his door.

'Everything all right, Clyde?' she asked quietly.

'Yes, why wouldn't it be?'

'What was that all about earlier? You know, with that Greg?'

'It wasn't about anything,' frowned Clyde. 'He does youth work. Sometimes we go to youth club and he's there. That's it.'

'Rick and Kevin don't like him, though.'

'It's up to them who they like or don't like,' Clyde answered. 'It's got nothing to do with me.'

'So why do you like him when they don't?' Ashley kept on.

Clyde was starting to feel uncomfortable. 'I never said I *did* like him.'

'You didn't have to. It's obvious you think he's OK. Otherwise you wouldn't have bothered to speak to him. Rick and Kevin didn't.' Ashley paused. 'It's a shame, really.'

'What d'you mean?' demanded Clyde. 'What's a shame?'

'Rick and Kevin are good mates of yours, aren't they? I mean, you wouldn't want to upset them?'

'Course not.' Clyde didn't have a clue what Ashley was getting at.

'It's not a good idea, you know – getting friendly

with people your best friends don't like,' Ashley continued. 'Makes things awkward. Especially as he's a Topz and you guys are sworn enemies.'

Clyde shook his head. 'He's not a Topz.'

'But he's on Topz's side, isn't he? So it's the same thing.'

'Look,' Clyde said, 'he was just nice to me one day, that's all. I'm not making him my best mate instead of Dixons.'

'Yeah, I know,' smiled Ashley, but it was one of her cold smiles. 'It's just, *I've* shown your friends that I'll stick up for them. I got Topz out of the park that afternoon, didn't I? They know they can rely on me. If *they* hate Topz, *I* hate Topz …' She stopped again and shook her head. 'I'm just not so sure about you.'

'What do you mean by that?' Clyde could feel his skin beginning to prickle.

'I *mean*,' said Ashley slowly, 'that it's hard to trust someone when you're not sure whose side they're on. Are you on Dixons' side, Clyde?'

'Of course I am! I *am* a Dixon, aren't I?' Clyde was growing more and more flustered. It was almost as if he'd done something wrong and Ashley was cross with him. He didn't want that. He wanted Ashley to go on thinking he was a good kid. He wanted Ashley to keep being proud of him – keep making him feel good about himself. 'Look,' he mumbled, 'I'm sorry if I spoke to Greg, all right? But if you don't want me to, I'll never speak to him again. I'll keep out of his way.'

'That'd be good,' nodded Ashley. 'But it's not about what *I* want, is it? I think you need to prove yourself to your friends. Show them that you still hate Topz as much as ever.'

'What are you talking about? I *do* hate them!' Clyde gulped. 'How am I supposed to *prove* it?'

Ashley gazed at him. 'I'll have a think about that,' she said finally. 'When I've come up with some ideas, I'll let you know. All right, Clyde?'

She turned away, walked out of the room and closed the door behind her. She was smiling again, but this time not at Clyde. Ashley was feeling triumphant. In control. In a few short weeks, she had managed to turn Clyde's hatred towards her into admiration. She'd persuaded Clyde that she really liked her little brother. That she was glad they were a family.

In fact, Ashley had reached a point where she was fairly sure she could get Clyde to do anything she wanted him to.

Back in her own bedroom, Ashley pulled a pad of paper and a pen from the drawer of her desk. At the top of the page, she wrote a heading in capital letters:

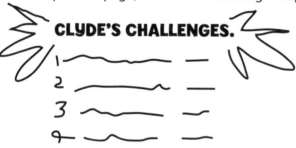

CLYDE'S CHALLENGES.

1 —————— —
2 —————— —
3 ———— —
4 ——— —

Twelve

Greg had a prayer list. A typed list of people's names and events going on that he wanted to remember to pray for. It was fixed to a corkboard above his desk at home, with a drawing pin at each corner. He printed out a fresh one every week. Sometimes the names and events changed, but what Greg wanted to talk to God about most always went at the very top.

Topping the list that Greg had just pinned up this week was the name, 'Clyde Bicton'.

Clyde had been somewhere on Greg's prayer list ever since their chat on the bench at the shopping centre. Greg prayed for Clyde when he wasn't on his list, too. When he started chatting to God, lots of different people and things would crop up. Dixons were there more often than not.

But sometimes, if Greg felt worried about a particular person, or found they kept popping into his head, he knew it was God nudging him to pray for them especially.

It was like that with Clyde. Recently, at some point or other through the day, he found that the Dixons boy was on his mind.

Greg stood back from the corkboard and gazed at his latest prayer list thoughtfully. Then, after a moment, he picked up a pen and wrote a Bible verse next to Clyde's name: *'You are my hiding place'* (Psalm 32:7).

God had been Greg's hiding place for as long as he could remember. Greg knew that when he went to God with a problem or a worry, then God would help him. God would take care of him. He was always there. He listened when Greg talked to Him. He answered his prayers, too. Perhaps not always in the way Greg was expecting, but always in the best way. Greg felt safe every day just knowing that God was with him.

When life was difficult, *God* was Greg's hiding place.

And Greg knew that what Clyde desperately needed was to discover for himself that God could be his hiding place, too.

Ashley hadn't made *her* list yet. In her desk drawer was the piece of paper with the heading, **CLYDE'S CHALLENGES**, but there was nothing written on it. Her plan was to note down each challenge as Clyde completed it. She knew her younger half-brother would do whatever she told him to. She'd made sure of that.

It was Saturday morning. Topz were in the park before Dixons. Benny, John, Josie and Danny were playing football. A couple of hours before, it had been pouring with rain. The weather forecast for nearly the whole weekend was wet, wet and more wet. Now, the four of them were out making the most of a short dry spell before the next cloudburst.

Dixons and Ashley had had the same idea. They zoomed in through the park gates on their skateboards. When Kevin spotted Topz, he made a face.

'Why can't this park be a Topz-free zone?' he scowled. 'They're always here. They think they own the place.'

Rick nudged Ashley. 'Can you get rid of them again?' he asked, his eyes lighting up mischievously. 'Like you did before? You could say they're not allowed to play football in here any more. It's become a ball-free area, or something. You can get those, you know. I've seen signs in car parks.'

Ashley sighed and gave a shrug. 'I suppose I could,' she replied, sounding as though she couldn't be bothered. 'Don't think they'll fall for the same sort of thing again, though, do you? Anyway it's boring me doing all the work. I think it's time we tried something different. Gave someone else a turn at being a hero.' She broke off and looked at Clyde pointedly. 'I reckon it should be you who gets rid of them today, Clyde.'

For a moment, Clyde was taken aback. He raised his eyebrows. 'How am I supposed to do that?'

'Think of something,' said Ashley, flatly. Then, leaning forward she whispered into Clyde's ear, 'Remember what we talked about? This is your chance to prove yourself. **Prove you're a *real* Dixon.**'

Clyde wanted to laugh, but Ashley's face was deadly serious. This was no joke.

'What are you whispering about?' Rick asked.

'Nothing,' said Ashley, her eyes still fixed on Clyde. 'Clyde and me just have a special understanding, don't we, Clyde?'

She watched him, waiting to see what he'd do next. She knew she'd made him feel uncomfortable. She also knew he'd do anything not to let her down.

Clyde's mind was blank. Dixons were always doing things to annoy Topz. Shouting at them; running through the middle of their football games; even kicking a ball at them when they went past on their bikes. It was a laugh. It was Dixons' way of showing off to each other as much as trying to wind up the Topz Gang.

This was different. This wasn't just Clyde and Dixons messing about. Ashley had told him it was time to prove himself. If he got it wrong, his big sister would be disappointed in him. Not only that, he'd end up looking like some sort of sad loser in front of his friends.

But what could he do? What could he possibly do …?

Clyde forced a grin. 'Maybe I *won't* get rid of them,' he said, trying to cover himself. 'Maybe I'll just wipe the stupid smiles off their stupid faces.'

He turned slowly and started to walk towards the little group of Topz who were still playing football some way ahead of him.

Josie spotted him first, but not before Benny had kicked the ball hard in her direction. It flew towards her, though she never saw it. Her eyes were fixed on the Dixons boy who was now running at them. As the ball sailed over her head and continued a way before hitting the ground, the Topz boys noticed Clyde, too.

Suddenly, Clyde changed direction. He wasn't heading straight for them any more. He was making for the ball. Even as he'd started towards Topz, Clyde still didn't know what he was going to do to spoil their game. It wasn't until he saw the football flying further and further away from the Topz Gang that he had the idea. It was so simple. Grab it! Run off with it so they couldn't play any more! He was much closer to it than they were. He'd also taken them by surprise. The ball was practically in his hands before Benny even started to chase him.

'No, Benny!' shouted Josie.

Benny took no notice. He'd come down to the park to play, hadn't he? He didn't want any trouble. But he could see exactly what the Dixons boy was going to do

– and he didn't see why he should have to stand there and let him run off with their football.

Benny tore across the grass as fast as he could. When he saw Clyde bend down and pick up the ball, he pushed himself even faster.

But instead of instantly running off now the football was in his grasp, all at once Clyde stopped and turned – just for a moment – which is when Benny saw the other Dixons. They were with the tall, blonde girl who seemed to like hanging around with them; the one who'd played that stupid prank about dogs not being allowed in the park.

Clyde waved at them, held the ball high above his head like a trophy and jumped in the air, whooping with delight. The next moment he'd burst into a run again. In the distance, Rick and Kevin cheered excitedly. Ashley was watching, too, but in silence.

Benny looked back at Clyde. He was still running, but not towards Dixons. Where was he going? As Benny swivelled round to head after him, he lost his footing on the wet ground and fell with a dull smack. It was a soft landing but only because the rain had turned everything to mud. When he scrambled back upright, he was plastered in it.

Clyde, meanwhile, had just reached the park gates and disappeared through them. Danny and John began to chase after him. Only half-heartedly, though. They had seen the audience of Dixons, too. They wanted their football back, but if they caught up with Clyde and tried to get it back from him, they didn't like to think what Kevin and Rick might do.

'He can't *do* that!' yelled Benny. 'He can't just run off with our ball. I'm going after him.'

'No, Benny,' said Josie firmly. 'The others are watching. That girl's with them as well.'

'I don't care!' Benny snapped. 'We try to do what Greg says and keep out of their way, but it's impossible. They don't try to keep out of *our* way. They're always messing with us. Especially Clyde! I've been praying for him, too, but he's still mean. Why doesn't God stop him wrecking everything? It's like He doesn't even care!'

'Come on Benny, you don't really mean that,' said John. He and Danny had given up any idea of getting their ball back.

'Yes, I do, John!' shouted Benny. 'Why doesn't God *do* something?' Wiping his muddy hands on his even muddier hoodie, he turned his back on his friends and marched off out of the park.

Clyde watched him go. He was hiding in a phone box just beyond the entrance gates. Still clutching the football, he gasped for breath from his sprint out of the park. The phone box gave him a good view of the park gates and he gazed at them, willing Topz to appear. When he saw Benny storming through, he could hardly believe his eyes. He'd done it! He'd got rid of the Gang! Quickly, he huddled down further to make sure he wouldn't be spotted.

Another few moments passed. Clyde didn't take his eyes off the gateway. Where were the other Topz? He'd expected them to be following hot on Benny's heels, but there was no sign of them. Why had they decided to stay when Benny had gone?

Clyde stood up a little to get a better view. Almost instantly, he ducked back down. There they were! John, Danny and Josie, walking slowly out of the park with their heads down. They didn't look as if they were having the best of mornings. In fact they looked miserable.

'**Yesss!**' Clyde hissed to himself. He started to grin delightedly. He'd wiped the smiles clean off Topz's faces just as he'd told Dixons he would. More importantly, he'd got rid of them from the park, exactly as Ashley had challenged him to.

Clyde was certain to be back in his big sister's good books now, wasn't he?

After all, he'd done what Ashley had said: he'd just proved himself.

Thirteen

When Ashley and Clyde got home, the first thing Ashley did was to go up to her room and close the door. She took the piece of paper headed CLYDE'S CHALLENGES and spread it out on her desk.

Taking a pen, she wrote, **'Get rid of Topz'**.

Ashley felt pleased. Not with Clyde because he had completed the challenge successfully. Ashley was pleased with herself. She wanted Clyde to do whatever she told him to, and that morning, Clyde had done exactly that.

When Clyde ran back into the park with his trophy football after Topz had left, Kevin and Rick had cheered him again, but Ashley was still oddly quiet. She hardly spoke all the way home. That's not what Clyde was expecting. He thought Ashley would pat him on the back, tell him he'd done well and say that she was proud of him.

But Ashley didn't do any of those things. She hardly looked at Clyde at all.

She simply said, 'I'm bored now. Let's go.'

Clyde couldn't understand it. How could Ashley still be cross with him when he'd done exactly what she wanted?

On the landing, he hovered outside her bedroom. He wondered whether to knock on the door. What could he have done wrong this time? He was desperate to know.

Suddenly, Ashley pulled the door open. Her eyes narrowed when she looked at Clyde, but she didn't seem surprised to see him. It was as if she knew he'd be there.

'Why are you hanging around out here, Clyde? Are you spying on me?'

'No, 'course not,' Clyde muttered, shaking his head. 'I wouldn't spy on you, would I? Why would you think that?'

Ashley shrugged. 'It's hard to trust anyone, isn't it?' she said quietly. 'Even in your own family.'

'Not even me?'

'Not even you, Clyde.'

'I got Topz out of the park though, didn't I?' Clyde stumbled on. 'You told me to prove myself and I have. Kevin and Rick know exactly whose side I'm on now. They loved what I did, too, didn't they? They were cheering! Did you see those Topz's faces when I nicked their ball? ... You know whose side I'm on now, too ... don't you?'

Clyde's voice trailed off. He peered into Ashley's face, anxiously trying to find some sign of approval. Anything that would show him that Ashley was pleased with her little brother for completing her challenge; that she was proud of him again.

Ashley didn't answer. There was what seemed like a long, empty silence.

Finally she said, 'So you got Topz out of the park. It's no big deal, is it? Anyone could have done what you did.'

Clyde felt his stomach twist. How was this possible? He hadn't won Ashley's praise at all, had he? Far from it. Ashley seemed to think even less of him now. Worst of all, as Clyde stared into his half-sister's eyes, he spotted something he recognised: disappointment. The same disappointment he seemed to see when his dad looked at him.

'I don't understand,' Clyde gulped. 'What have I done wrong? I did what you said. Why are you still cross?'

'I'm not cross,' Ashley replied. 'Why do you say that?

It's just that we're not done, that's all.'

'What d'you mean?'

'We're not done, are we?' Ashley repeated. 'You completed a challenge today – hip hip hooray! But I've got more than one challenge for you to do, Clyde. You haven't proved yourself yet. Not to anybody. And who knows if you'll be able to do what I ask you to tomorrow?'

'I will!' Clyde blurted out. 'I can do anything you tell me to! I can!'

Ashley gave him one last look – almost as if she felt sorry for him, Clyde thought. Then she ambled past and went downstairs.

In his bedroom, Clyde threw himself onto his bed. Everything had been different lately. Things had been good. He'd been feeling so much better about himself. Ashley wasn't just his half-sister, she'd become a friend, too. The sort of friend Greg had talked to him about. A friend he could trust, who would listen to him and help him out. A friend he wanted to impress. What had happened? How could it all have gone so wrong?

Clyde rolled over and hugged his knees in tightly to his stomach. He hurt inside. He didn't want things to be like this. He wanted to make them right again. But how? Especially when he didn't understand what it was he'd done wrong.

Bullying was something Clyde knew a lot about. After all, he'd been a bully for most of his life. He never cared how much he upset the person he was picking on. Why should he? He just enjoyed the feeling of being in control; of scaring someone. He liked how powerful it made him feel.

But, for the first time ever, Clyde was getting to know

what it felt like to be the victim. Although he didn't realise what was happening, Clyde was being bullied by Ashley. It made him feel weak, and even more worthless and miserable.

All he wanted now was to stop hurting. But that wasn't going to happen any time soon.

Ashley didn't mention challenges to Clyde the next day. Or the day after that. She didn't talk to Clyde much at all.

'What's up with you two?' their dad asked. He'd been pleased with how well his kids had been getting on since the first few awkward days – pleased and surprised. So what was going on now?

'Nothing's up, Dad,' smiled Ashley. 'We're all right, aren't we, Clyde?'

'Yeah, of course we are,' Clyde mumbled back.

As he looked at Ashley, he hoped that perhaps they *were* all right; that maybe Ashley had just been in a bad mood and now she was feeling better. But one glance at her empty smile told him that nothing had changed.

Later that day, Clyde said, 'I'm still waiting for another challenge, Ashley. Have you come up with something yet? I'm ready when you are.'

Ashley shook her head. 'I've got more important things to do than sit around coming up with challenges for you.'

Towards the end of the week, Clyde tried again. 'What if we come up with some challenges together? I bet I could think of some awesome stuff to do.'

'What would be the point in setting your own challenges?' Ashley frowned. 'Besides, I've got one for you.'

'Cool! What is it?'

'Don't ask me about challenges again.'

'What?' Clyde looked confused.

'That's your challenge,' sighed Ashley. 'Not to ask me about challenges any more. I'm sick of you going on about them.'

Clyde disappeared up to his room and sat with his back against the closed door. *Don't ask me about challenges again.* That was a harder challenge than getting Topz out of the park! How could Clyde not ask? Everything was weird with Ashley all the time. Up in the air. He wanted so much for it all to go back to normal. He couldn't think about anything else.

How much longer would he have to wait?

Clyde wasn't the only one who knew about bullying. Benny did, too. He'd been picked on at school when he was younger. And these days Dixons hardly ever missed an opportunity to get at the Topz Gang. So Benny understood exactly the hurt that Clyde was feeling.

What he didn't realise was that Clyde was feeling it.

When Benny went to bed that night, he was still in a bad mood.

'What's with the grumpy face?' his dad had asked him several times.

'I haven't got a grumpy face,' Benny growled back. 'I'm just thinking, that's all.'

'Well, they must be very grumpy thoughts,' replied his dad. 'Come on, cheer up! You're scaring the goldfish.'

Benny gave him a sideways look. 'Dad, we haven't got any goldfish.'

'Haven't we? Well, I expect they've all moved out so they don't have to look at your grumpy face.'

But not even Benny's dad could get him to smile.

There was a part of Benny that wondered whether he should simply to come out with it and tell his parents: 'Dixons have stolen our football.' It's just that if he did, his dad was quite likely to march straight round to Clyde's house and demand the ball back. And that's not what Benny wanted. This was about more than just a football. He longed to show Clyde and the other Dixons that they couldn't keep on being mean; that it was time their nastiness stopped. For good. The problem was ... how?

'I'm sorry I'm angry, God ...'

Benny stopped. Quite often his prayers seemed to start with 'I'm sorry I'm angry'. And when he thought about it, the reason he was angry was usually to do with Dixons.

I hate this feeling. And it's not even my fault. It's Dixons. It's always Dixons that make me feel this way. All we were doing was playing football, and they couldn't leave us alone. At least Clyde couldn't.

They were all in it, though. They were all watching. Rick and Kevin – and that other one. That older girl. As if three Dixons isn't enough, now there seem to be four of them!

Why doesn't it ever change, God? Topz all pray for Dixons. Not every day, maybe, but we do talk to You about them. I've been talking to You about Clyde lots.

So has Greg. Greg told me he's put Clyde at the top of his prayer list. That means he must be talking to You about him at least three times a day. That's what Greg does with the people who are top of his prayer list. I said to him once, 'Doesn't God get bored hearing the same prayer over and over and over again?' But Greg said no. He said the more often we talk to You about something, the more serious You know we are about it. He said we mustn't give up either. Even if nothing seems to change, we have to keep on asking You. We have to trust You that You'll answer the prayer when it's the right time.

So, I'm not giving up, God. I'm really not. But how much longer till You **do** something about Dixons? Don't You care that they're so mean to us? Don't You care that Clyde tried to break my bike and now he's pinched our football? It's not fair. I know You **do** care because You love us. You love everyone, even Dixons. But that's what I don't understand. If You love them, why don't You help them to find You? To make friends with You?

Greg says we'll never understand everything about You. He says if we could, that would probably make You just like us, and then You wouldn't be God. And He says You never force anyone to be Your friend. You want people to love You because they **want** to love You. Well, I'm really glad You're God and everything, and I'm even gladder that You're my Friend. Must be rubbish being a Dixon and not being friends with You like that. I just wish I knew what to do.

Is there something You want me to do, God? If there is,

I'll do it, I really will. It's just that I don't know how to do anything for Dixons. I can't talk to them about You because almost every time I see them, they do something horrible and then all I want to do is shout at them. I don't want to be 'loving', that's for dead certain.

You're the One who's loving, God, so please do something. I've been asking and asking but nothing's changed. What are You waiting for? When are all my prayers going to make a difference?

Fourteen

Greg had overslept. It didn't happen often. Two or three times a year perhaps. But he'd slept really badly that Saturday night; just couldn't get comfortable. When he finally dropped off, he must have gone into a very deep sleep because he didn't hear his alarm. On Sunday mornings he was usually up at seven o'clock. That gave him plenty of time to get organised for church and for leading Sunday Club.

The first thing he saw when he opened his eyes on this particular Sunday morning was the half-empty mug of tea he'd made in the middle of the night. The next was his alarm clock – which told him disapprovingly that it was almost eight.

What? No, no, no! How could it be eight o'clock? Greg leapt out of bed and hurled himself into the shower. After a quick dry off, he pulled on his dressing gown and rushed downstairs to the kitchen. Dropping a couple of pieces of bread in the toaster, he shot back up to his bedroom to get dressed.

By the time he was back in the kitchen, the toast had popped up ready for a spreading of butter and marmalade. Greg ate it speedily, chewing on mouthfuls in between stapling together worksheets for this morning's Sunday Club and putting them in his bag. He got marmalade on a couple of pages but he was sure his Sunday Clubbers wouldn't mind. They'd probably find the idea of Greg oversleeping hilarious.

Greg had just got to his front door and pulled it open ready to leave when he realised he hadn't combed his hair. He glanced quickly in the hall mirror.

Perhaps it didn't look too bad. Slinging his bag over his shoulder, he raked his fingers through it. Better than nothing, he thought.

That's when he remembered the other thing he'd forgotten. Orange squash. There was none left in Sunday Club's refreshment cupboard. If Greg had been up at seven, he'd have had plenty of time to go to church via the corner shop to buy some. Having to do that now would make him even later. Driving in the car wouldn't help because it would take him ages to find somewhere to park.

Nothing for it, then. He'd have to go on his bike. Greg didn't usually cycle to church on a Sunday. He walked. He didn't like riding his bike when he was carrying a heavy bag full of stuff for Sunday Club. It would be even heavier this morning with a bottle of orange squash in it. But he had no choice. It was either that or be late. He checked that he had his wallet with him. Then he lifted the strap of his bag over his head to the opposite shoulder so that it hung across his body. That way it wouldn't slip off as he cycled along.

His bike stood right next to him by the front door. It always lived in the hall. Greg didn't have a shed to keep it in. If he'd been out riding in the rain, he'd put newspaper down on the floor and stand it on that.

Outside, he pulled the front door shut, wheeled his bike to the gate, hopped on the saddle and pedalled off.

Ten minutes later, he was just coming out of the corner shop having bought the squash, when Ashley spotted him. She and Dixons were heading for the park.

'Isn't that your youth club leader?' Ashley asked, nodding her head in Greg's direction.

'He's not *our* youth club leader,' Rick scoffed. 'But yeah, that's him.'

As they got closer, they saw Greg stuff the bottle of squash into his bag, then turn his bike round. He was in such a hurry that he only noticed the four of them when he started to pedal away. Slowing just a little as he rode past, he called, 'Morning! Sorry, can't stop. Late for church!' Then he sped off.

'Cool bike,' Kevin remarked as he watched Greg disappear up the road.

'Very cool,' Ashley agreed. Her eyes were shining. An idea had occurred to her all of a sudden. She turned to face Clyde. 'Guess what, little brother,' she smirked. 'I've just thought up your next challenge.'

Ashley, Clyde, Rick and Kevin stood on the other side of the road from the church. Lots of people were arriving, walking up the steps and into the building through the wide double doors. No one seemed to take any notice of the boys and the tall girl watching them.

Different members of Topz turned up, too. Clyde watched with the others, but he didn't really see anything. His head was too full of the challenge Ashley had set him.

'We're all agreed Greg's got a cool bike, yeah?' Ashley had said near the corner shop, an impish look in her eyes.

'Yeah!' grinned Rick and Kevin.

She reached out and put an arm around Clyde's shoulders. 'Then, guess what I want you to do, Clyde?' she asked.

Clyde knew instantly. He just wanted more than anything to be wrong.

'What?' he gulped.

'You're going to go to church and pinch that bicycle.'

Standing opposite the church building, Clyde could feel himself sweating even though it was a damp, cold day. Under his hoodie, his T-shirt clung to his back. The inside of his mouth was dry as dust. His tongue felt odd and swollen. He couldn't swallow.

Of all the things Ashley could have asked him to do, why did it have to be this? Greg had been kind to him and Clyde really didn't want to steal from him. Besides, surely he'd never get away with it. Something small maybe – a book, a hat, an umbrella even. But Greg's *bike*?

Rick was fairly certain Greg usually parked the bike somewhere down the side of the church building. He'd seen him before, pushing it along the little alleyway between the church and the hall where they sometimes went for youth club.

There were fewer people arriving now. Just the odd one or two. The morning service must have been about to start.

When no one had come along for several minutes, Ashley said, 'OK, Clyde. You're on.'

'No.' Clyde shook his head. 'No, I'd better leave it a bit longer. At least wait till we can hear them all singing or something.'

Clyde badly wanted to please Ashley. He'd been waiting and waiting for another chance to show her that he was still a 'good kid', as Ashley used to call him. But at the same time, the longer he put off attempting this particular challenge, the more chance there was that Ashley might suddenly give him a grin and say,

'Clyde, I'm joking!' – wasn't there?

'Trouble is, Clyde,' Ashley sighed, 'I'm getting bored just hanging around here. What about you two?' She looked at Rick and Kevin.

'Yeah, go on, Clyde!' Rick grinned. 'Get on with it!'

Clyde didn't answer.

'What's the matter?' Ashley asked, head on one side as she gazed coldly at her half-brother. 'Not scared are you?'

That was the moment when Clyde knew there was nothing for it. Ashley wasn't joking. She wasn't going to change her mind. And if Clyde didn't do exactly as she said right there and then, he reckoned he'd probably lose her respect forever.

Clyde glanced up and down the street. There was no one around now. The flow of people into church had stopped. He waited for two cars to pass, one on each side of the road. Then, head down and heart pounding in his chest, he crossed over to the church. At the entrance to the alleyway, he took a last look back at the little group watching him. Rick and Kevin gave him the thumbs up. Ashley just stared. Clyde was sure she was sneering at him.

Then he stepped in between the two buildings and lost sight of them.

There was no sign of the bike in the alleyway. In front of Clyde was what looked like a corridor, linking the church to the hall. Perhaps Greg kept his bike inside. There were windows in the corridor and a door at one end.

In one way, the windows were good. They meant Clyde could see in.

In another way, they were very bad. Anyone walking through the corridor would be able to look out and see *him*. He'd have to be quick.

Clyde ran forwards. When he was right up close to one of the windows, he crouched down.

So far, so good.

Now all he needed to do was raise his head up just enough to have a look through the glass. If the bike wasn't there, what then? He had to find it. He couldn't fail Ashley.

Resting his fingertips on the windowsill to help him balance, Clyde stretched his head up.

And there the bike was! Leaning up against the corridor wall right in front of him.

Clyde was almost relieved. At least he'd found it. The bad news was that now he had to get inside the corridor and steal it. He could feel the sweat prickling across his forehead. He was sticky and uncomfortable all over. But it didn't matter. It *couldn't* matter. The only way he was going to be able to complete his challenge was to focus on what he was doing. On every single footstep.

Clyde turned slightly and his gaze fell on the door. Still crouching, he made sure he kept his head below window level as he slid himself towards it. He reached out for the handle. What if the door was locked? What was he supposed to do then? Break in? He was certain Ashley would settle for nothing less.

Clyde bobbed up for one more look inside to check there was no one about. Then, slowly but firmly, he pushed down on the handle.

The door swung open.

Yes! He was inside!

There was the sound of singing from the direction of the church, but he hardly heard it. It was mostly drowned out by the thudding of his heart which seemed to throb in his ears.

There was no lock on the bike. Clyde saw that in a second. What a relief. At least he wouldn't have to carry it. It was facing the wrong way and there wasn't room to turn it round, so he'd have to edge it out backwards, but that wasn't a problem. Not like a lock would have been.

Clyde gulped hard. Any minute now, he would have backed the bike out through the doorway and down the alleyway – and Ashley would see what he'd done! Ashley would see him standing there with Greg's bike! She'd realise that Clyde wasn't just a 'good' kid, he was a *'great'* kid! She'd understand that Clyde would do anything for his big sister. Anything to win her admiration. And because Clyde had done something so daring, Ashley would give it wholeheartedly. Of course she would!

The trouble was, it wasn't Ashley who saw him with the bike first.

Clyde had only just managed to get the back wheel out through the doorway when another door opened. The door at the far end of the corridor that led into the hall. Hearing the hinges squeak, Clyde's head whipped around.

The boy standing there looked just as shocked as he did. **It was Benny.**

Fifteen

Neither Clyde nor Benny moved. They stood frozen, staring at each other. Benny could hardly believe his eyes. Clyde didn't know what to say. What to do. It was obvious he was trying to make off with the bike. There was no point pretending he wasn't. Maybe he should just drop it and run. After all, it was only Benny. Clyde was sure he could outrun him, no problem. Ashley would understand, wouldn't she? He'd been caught and he had to get out of there.

Only suddenly, it wasn't just Benny. Greg's voice drifted through the open door from the hall.

'Thanks for your help, Benny. That'll teach me to oversleep ...'

Greg stopped speaking abruptly as he appeared in the doorway. His eyes flicked from Clyde's face to the bike, and back again.

'Hello, Clyde,' he said finally. 'Where are you off to – with my bike?'

Benny was still stunned. This was shocking, even for a Dixon. It was one thing picking on other kids. It was quite another stealing a bike from a grown-up. And not just any grown-up, either, but Greg. Greg was good to Dixons.

Clyde was still staring. His blue eyes looked huge and his face was white under his thick hair. Although he was sweating, he felt freezing cold. As he gripped the bike, he began to shiver.

'It's all right, Clyde,' Greg said gently. 'Put the bike back where it was, and let's go and have a chat.'

Benny frowned. 'Have a chat? Aren't you going to

do something? Clyde's a thief. Shouldn't you phone the police?'

Before Greg had time to answer, Clyde panicked. He let go of the bike. Twisting round, he tried to make a run for it. But rather than falling the other way, the bike toppled over onto him. The sleeve of his hoodie got caught on the handlebars. He yanked at it, but then he stumbled and tripped over one of the pedals. Suddenly, he was lying in a heap of arms and legs on the ground. The bike was on top of him, crushing him into the doorframe.

Instantly Greg was there. He lifted the bike off the terrified Dixon.

'Take it, would you, Benny?' he said.

Benny wheeled it out of the way and Greg bent down to help Clyde up. Clyde didn't look at him. He didn't move either. He just lay there, still shivering.

Greg gave him a half-smile. 'I'm not going to call the police, Clyde. But we are going to have that chat.'

Ashley, Rick and Kevin waited and waited. They kept their eyes fixed on the entrance to the alleyway. Clyde didn't appear.

'Where is he?' frowned Kevin. 'How long does it take to nick a bike? Greg said he was going to church. It must *be* there.'

'What if something's happened?' asked Rick.

'Like what?' Kevin grunted.

'Like what if he's got caught?'

There was a pause, then Ashley shrugged. 'If Clyde's got caught, that's *his* problem. Nothing to do with us.'

'Well, it sort of is,' muttered Rick.

'Why's that?' Ashley demanded.

Rick hesitated. 'Because you told him to go and pinch the bike.'

Ashley turned and gave him an icy glare. 'Not me, Rick. I never said a thing. What Clyde does is up to him. It's not *my* responsibility. He's on his own.'

With that, Ashley turned and started to walk away.

'Where are you going?' frowned Kevin.

'None of your business,' Ashley called back over her shoulder.

'But we can't just leave him there!'

Ashley turned. 'Why not? Like I said, Clyde's on his own.' She carried on walking. She didn't look at them again.

When she got home, the first thing her dad asked was, 'Where's Clyde?'

Ashley shook her head and shrugged. 'Don't know. He went off.'

Up in her bedroom, she went straight to her desk and pulled out the piece of paper with CLYDE'S CHALLENGES written at the top. She glanced at it for a moment. Then, as if she couldn't be bothered with it any more, she screwed the paper into a ball and dropped it in the wastepaper bin.

Standing at the window, Ashley looked out. There was still no sign of Clyde. He could be anywhere. With anyone. She wasn't worried what her little brother would say when he eventually showed up. Even if he told their dad what had really happened – that his half-sister had forced him to steal a bike – she knew Rob would never believe him.

What she didn't expect, however, was for Rob to

answer the front door bell some time after lunch to find Clyde standing there with Greg. Rob recognised Greg instantly as the youth leader from the church. But he was very surprised to see him with his son.

'Good afternoon, Mr Bicton,' Greg greeted him cheerfully.

'Hello,' Rob said, trying to keep the curiosity out of his voice. 'Is everything … all right?'

'Everything's great,' Greg replied. 'I've just been enjoying Clyde's company. Hope I haven't kept him out too long.'

Greg told Rob that he and Clyde had bumped into each other and had got talking. He didn't mention his bike. He didn't mention what they'd talked about, either. That was between him and Clyde.

After he'd picked Clyde up off the ground, Greg had asked Benny to go into church. Then he'd taken Clyde into the hall. He knew they didn't have long. Sunday Club would be starting soon.

But in those quiet moments before children started streaming out of the service, Greg told Clyde he wasn't cross with him. He was worried about him. If Clyde wanted to tell him what was going on, Greg said he'd try to help.

Just before Sunday Club began, Greg showed Clyde a tiny office.

'No one comes in here,' he said. 'Just me. You can wait here till I'm finished with the kids if you like. Then we can carry on chatting. Like I told you once before, talking really does help.'

Greg didn't honestly expect Clyde to stay. He imagined he'd probably run off the first chance he had. So when everyone had gone home and he found Clyde still sitting there, he was almost surprised. But at the same time, Clyde was at the very top of his prayer list. Greg had been talking to God about him every day. Almost from the moment he'd seen the Dixons boy trying to steal his bike, Greg was fairly sure God had something in mind.

They talked for ages. Clyde told Greg all about Ashley: how he used to hate her because she always seemed to be his dad's favourite. But how he'd started to feel differently about her once she'd actually moved to Holly Hill. Kevin and Clyde thought Ashley was awesome. After a while, Clyde had begun to think so, too. And when Ashley told her little brother that she was proud of him, Clyde had suddenly started to feel on top of the world. Maybe he *was* worth something after all. Did it really matter if he was always second best as far as his dad was concerned? Ashley, the coolest kid in Holly Hill, thought Clyde was great.

But then everything had changed. It was as if Ashley had got tired of him. Bored. Clyde tried to explain to Greg that all he wanted was to get his big sister's approval back. He couldn't understand why he'd lost it. He just needed Ashley to be his friend again. That was why, when Ashley began to set him challenges, Clyde knew he had to go through with them to prove himself to her.

So even before Clyde told Greg it was Ashley who wanted him to steal the bike, Greg knew.

'You should never, ever let yourself be pushed into something you don't want to do,' Greg said. 'And doing something wrong to get someone else's approval – well, that approval's just not worth having. Do you want to know what I found out a long time ago? The only approval that really matters is God's. So if you want to set out to make someone happy, try to make God happy. He *loves* you and He'll never hurt you. He made you, Clyde. He thinks you're amazing. That should make you feel like a million zillion pounds!' Greg paused. 'No. That should make you feel priceless …'

Clyde wasn't the only one Greg wanted to have a chat with. He needed to talk to Benny, too; to ask him to keep praying for Clyde. When he left the Dixons Estate a little later that afternoon, he walked straight round to Benny's flat. The two of them talked for a long while before Greg finally went home.

After he'd gone, Benny still had plenty to say.

It's me again, God, and guess what I'm talking about? Clyde. Again.

Greg says he knows I'm angry because of all the nasty stuff Clyde's done. Especially just lately. But he says I have to keep praying for him. Greg says what's happened today is incredible, and it **is**! *Greg got to tell Clyde that You love him! And Clyde sat and listened! Clyde! From Dixons! Only You could have done that, God. Clyde was going to do something really bad today, and You've turned it into something really good.*

Greg can't tell me much. He says it wouldn't be fair and what Clyde told him has to stay just between the two of them. But he did tell me what I could pray for. He said that there are times for everyone when we need to

*know that we're safe. He said that what Clyde needs to
know more than anything today is how much You love
him, God. How much You want to take care of him.*

*There's this verse in the Bible. Greg says he's had it in his
head all week. 'You are my hiding place.' He says that's
what Clyde needs to understand. That he doesn't have
to let himself be pushed around. He needs to remember
that You are his hiding place. You are his safe place to
go when things are difficult. He can talk to You. He can
ask You to help him. He can ask You to stay right by his
side. And You will, God, because that's what You do.
But we have to trust You.*

*Can't really imagine anyone being able to push Clyde
around. I don't know who'd dare. I think it might be
something to do with that girl we keep seeing him with.
Greg says she's Clyde's half-sister and she's come to live
with them. So maybe she's not another Dixon after all.*

*Anyway, Greg reckons Clyde's problems aren't going to
go away. But he says You can help him deal with them.
So please, God, please help Clyde to start trusting You.
Help him to find You and to realise that all You want
is to be his friend. Please be his hiding place when he
needs to feel safe.*

*I asked Greg if he thought all our prayers would make
a difference to Clyde soon. He said we can't ever know
that. All we can do is wait – and keep talking to You.*

'Benny?'

It was his mum's voice. She was outside his bedroom.

Benny opened the door.

'There's someone to see you, Benny. It's one of those Dixons.'

Benny frowned. That couldn't be right. His mum must have got it wrong. Why would a Dixon be coming to see him? Dixons *never* called on Topz. It just didn't happen.

Cautiously, Benny walked along the hall. His mum followed a little way behind.

At the front door was Clyde. He stood there looking fidgety and awkward. In his hands was a football. Topz's football. The one he'd run off with that day in the park when Ashley had told him to get rid of the Topz Gang.

Clyde didn't say a word. He just bounced the ball on the floor once, caught it with both hands and held it out to Benny.

Benny took it. **'Erm ... thanks,'** he said.

Then the Dixons boy turned and walked away.

More SECRET STORIES!

Why not try the others in the series?

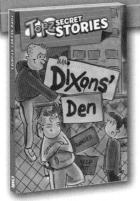

Dixons' Den
New to Holly Hill, Saf befriends Kevin 'the Dixon', who shows her the secret Dixons' den. Furious with Saf, the other Dixons make trouble. Can Saf trust anyone anymore? Can she trust God?

ISBN: 978-1-85345-690-9

Dixons and the Wolf
Rick the Dixon convinces Sarah from the Topz Gang to keep a secret. Rick needs help to look after Wolf the dog. Sarah agrees but she's worried. Is Rick telling the truth about Wolf?

ISBN: 978-1-85345-691-6

Pantomime Pandemonium
Topz plan to put on an open-air pantomime in aid of a local charity, but when Dixons decide to run an event the same day, Sarah loses her temper ... and may start losing friends too.

ISBN: 978-1-85345-916-0

For current prices, visit **www.cwr.org.uk/store**
Available online or from Christian bookshops.

Boys Only and Just for Girls

These special editions of *Topz Secret Diaries* will help you discover things about yourself and God with questions and quizzes, engaging puzzles, word searches, doodles, lists to write and more.

Topz Secret Diaries:
Boys Only
ISBN: 978-1-85345-596-4
126-page paperbacks,
129x197mm

Topz Secret Diaries:
Just for Girls
ISBN: 978-1-85345-597-1
126-page paperbacks,
129x197mm

Benny's Barmy Bits
ISBN: 978-1-85345-431-8

Danny's Daring Days
ISBN: 978-1-85345-502-5

Dave's Dizzy Doodles
ISBN: 978-1-85345-552-0

Gruff & Saucy's
Topzy-Turvy Tales
ISBN: 978-1-85345-553-7

John's Jam-Packed Jottings
ISBN: 978-1-85345-503-2

Josie's Jazzy Journal
ISBN: 978-1-85345-457-8

Paul's Potty Pages
ISBN: 978-1-85345-456-1

Sarah's Secret Scribblings
ISBN: 978-1-85345-432-5

Go to **www.cwr.org.uk/store**,
call 01252 784700
or visit a Christian bookshop.

Topz is a colourful daily devotional for 7- to 11-year-olds.

In each issue the Topz Gang teach children biblical truths through word games, puzzles, riddles, cartoons, competitions, simple prayers and daily Bible readings.

Available as an annual subscription
£15.95 (6 bimonthly issues includes p&p)
or as single issues **£2.95**.

Go to **www.cwr.org.uk/store**,
call 01252 784700 or visit a Christian bookshop.

Prices correct at time of printing.